# HOLLOW COVE PROMISES

# Leigh Allen

# Copyright

Hollow Cove Promises is a work of fiction. All names, characters, locations, and incidents are the products of the author's imagination or are used fictitiously. Any resemblance to actual events, locales, or persons, living or dead, is entirely coincidental.

HOLLOW COVE PROMISES: A NOVEL



Editing by Literary Edits

# Table of Contents

# 1

## *Mia*

"What the hell are you doing?"

I hear his voice behind me, but I don't bother turning to face my brother, Isaac. I am too busy painting one wall black in my bedroom to argue with him now.

Over the last year, I had been a little difficult to live with. That is, until I met Seth Parker. After my parents died at the beginning of my freshman year of high school, my world had been completely flipped upside down. Isaac had done his best to raise me while trying to live his own life too. Now, I had Seth and my best friend Grace. Without them, I wasn't sure where I would be right now.

"I am painting," I say, dipping the brush back into the paint can before smearing more black paint over my once gray wall.

"Yeah, no shit. Why?" he bellows.

Sighing, I turn and face my angry older brother, Isaac. "Because, now I can hang up all of my paintings and this black backdrop will make them look awesome," I stated, like he was crazy not to understand.

"Whatever," he mumbled. "I have to get to class. Just don't make too big a mess," he says, before retreating out the door.

Thankfully, Isaac found a way to still attend college classes in the evenings so he can finish his law degree. And, it gives me more time to sneak my boyfriend in while he is gone.

I finish the rest of the paint and then clean up my mess before showering.

When I emerged from my bathroom, I almost screamed when I found a beautiful boy sitting on my bed.

"Damn, took you long enough," Seth says, with his infamous smirk lighting up the room.

To say that smile does crazy things to my mind and body, is an understatement. Ever since Seth and I had made our relationship official, we had been attached at the hip. He had become my light in a time of darkness. My rock when I needed to find solid ground. He was my everything and I loved him more than I ever could have imagined.

It's not to say that our relationship has been easy. Truth be told, the start of us together was a complete shit show. A disaster of epic proportions.

Seth had been so ashamed of his past, he wanted to keep us a secret from the rest of Hollow Cove, the small town where we both lived. Then once we were both ok going public, everything exploded when Britley, Seth's once sister-in-law had been blackmailing him for money, claiming to be pregnant with his late brother, Alex's baby. It was all like something out of a terrible soap opera show, but it had been our life.

Now, we were both enjoying being in love in Hollow's Cove with no more drama in our way. At least for now anyway.

I saunter over to Seth and wrap my arms around his neck. "You have been working on that bike all day. You should have been here ten minutes ago," I argue.

Seth also loves art like me, that is one passion we both share. Besides one another. Seth has been obsessed with the Raven's Boy's Club for as long as he can remember. He wanted nothing more than to be part of their club and to feel part of their family.

"If I had known you had missed me so much, I would have gotten over here much faster," he moans, as he begins to nibble on my ear.

I close my eyes and enjoy the feel of his lips on my skin. This is what I love most about me and Seth. When we are together, everything else in the world just seems to fade away. Only the two of us matter.

Suddenly, a ding from my dresser alerts me to a text message. We both groan as our moment has been interrupted.

"Ignore it," Seth says, as his hands travel up and down my body.

"Glady," I smile, as I kiss Seth.

Next thing I know, my phone is now ringing and I know that whoever it is, isn't going to let up.

"Ugh, just answer it," Seth says, throwing his hands up in the air as he falls to the bed.

I rush over to the dresser, ready to curse at whoever is destroying my moment with Seth.

"What?" I bark out, when I answer the phone.

"Well, hello to you too," Grace laughs.

Grace is my best friend and the only other person in the world who can piss me off but still somehow make me love her.

"What is so important that you are blowing up my phone?" I ask, clearly annoyed.

"I have very important news to share," Grace says, her voice growing serious.

"Is everything ok?" I ask, now feeling like a jerk for being so rude. Maybe someone in her family was hurt, or worse.

"Yes, it's about school," Grace begins. "Apparently, there is a new boy in town. My social media pages were going crazy today with alerts that a new boy was seen moving into the old Hammond place," Grace almost yells.

I wish she were here right now in front of me, I would totally slap her.

"Seriously? That is what is so important?" I ask.

"Well, yes. And, he is apparently part of a motorcycle club from his last town. He rides a bike and everything," she whistles.

Now, this has my attention. "Why would I care about that?" I ask.

Seth, now seeing my interest in the conversation, sits up on my bed and watches me with intent.

"What is it?" he whispers to me.

I pull my phone away from my ear for a moment. "Apparently, there is a new kid in Hollow's Cove, and he was part of another motorcycle club," I say.

Seth's eyes rise as he thinks this over. The last motorcycle gang in Hollow's Cove was run by this sleezy guy named Charlie. The Raven's Boys and him had a dangerous rivalry that ended with Charlie going to jail. This could be a good or bad thing. I dreaded the thought.

"Are you even listening to me?" Grace yells into the phone.

"Yes," I say, rolling my eyes.

"Whatever. Anyway, I am coming over tonight to watch movies and eat our weight in pizza. Enjoy your time with Seth now, because you owe me a girls night. We can talk more about the gossip then," Grace says, before hanging up the phone.

I shake my head as I place the phone back onto my dresser. That girl is crazy, but I love her anyway.

"So, why does Grace care so much about some new kid coming to town?" Seth asks.

"How should I know, it's Grace. She's coming over tonight so I guess I will get more news," I say.

"Fine, but you are mine until then," Seth growls, grabbing me around the waist and pulling me onto his lap.

I straddle his waist as he pulls us both down onto the bed. Seth begins to remove my clothes slowly, one piece at a time as he enjoys every second of pleasuring my body. And with just one touch of his hands on my body, all thoughts escape my mind. Right now, all that matters is me and Seth. Everything else can wait.

# 2

*Seth*

I left Mia's house with a smile on my face.

I could hear the girls giggling inside as I walked down the stone path that led to the driveway. My bike sat under the streetlamp and damn it looked good. I admired the paint and custom design I had done just last week with my best friend Brody. He was part of the Raven's Boys's Club and I was still trying to work my way into their elusive and highly respected group. Doing custom work for the guys was just one step closer to being part of the family they created. A family I desperately wanted. Don't get me wrong, Mia has become my family now, but being in the Raven's Boys could open up doors for my future with Mia. A future I planned to have forever with her.

I threw my leg over my bike and began to rev the engine. Just as I started the second love of my life, I felt my phone vibrate in my pocket. I smiled, expecting to see a text from Mia. Maybe she'd decided to dump her best friend and invite me back in.

Only, when I looked down I got another good surprise. Not as good as knowing I would be having sex with my super hot girlfriend again, but still, good news.

Brody: Race tomorrow night behind the bar.

Me: What bar?

I was messing with Brody. We both knew exactly what bar he was talking about. The Raven's Boys Bar, which his oldest brother owned.

Brody: Stop being a jackass. Be there at nine.

Me: Definitely.

Brody: Rumor is, some guys with big money will be there betting, if you want in on it.

Me: Count me in.

Brody, my best friend and guy lucky enough to hold the last name Raven, had gotten into racing souped up cars lately. While his brothers were all big into their motorcycles like me, Brody preferred the speed of a fast car. Now, he had even started illegally drag racing and was making some big bucks.

Being that I had a pretty rough background, college wasn't in the picture for me. But, Mia was. And, I owed it to her to work my ass off to make a life she would be proud to have. We had overcome so much in our short time together, I wanted the rest of our lives to be easy.

I placed my phone back into my pocket and pulled out of Mia's driveway. Tomorrow, I will make a few thousand bucks.

# 3

## Mia

Thankfully, Isaac had started giving me the morning shifts on Saturday mornings, so I could have the evenings free with Seth. While he still wasn't excited about my relationship with Hollow Cove's very own bad boy, he was opening up to the idea more each day. That's all I could ask for, right?

I was busy wiping down the counter, when I heard the door chime go off. I looked up just in time to spot Grace strutting into the small shop.

"Hey girly, what's up?" she asked.

Grace had spent the night with me and then rushed home to go shopping with her mom. That was something I envied about her, she still had a mom to go shopping with. It was times like these that I felt that nagging pain in the pit of my stomach and I was reminded once again, that my parents were dead.

I forced a smile as I greeted my best friend.

"Hey," I offered.

"So, what are plans tonight?" she asked, raising her eyes at me.

"Um, not sure. I think Seth and I might hang out," I began.

Truth was, Grace had sort of become a third wheel lately. She wasn't dating anyone and now that I had Seth, she was not getting the hint that I needed my time alone with him, But, I didn't have the heart to tell her I didn't want her tagging along. I mean, it was Grace who had befriended me when I moved to Hollow Cove High School after my parents died. It was also Grace who had hung out with me when everyone else labeled me the school freak. I owed it to her. More importantly, I owed it to the both of us to find her a hot guy to start dating.

Before Grace could respond though, My eyes lit up like a kid at Christmas when I saw the hottest, sexiest, and most alluring male to ever walk the earth. Yes, Seth was entering the cafe and I already felt my body heating up with need.

"Hey girls, I have plans for us tonight," Seth smirked, as he straddled one of the bar stools and sat down in front of me.

Grace laughed as she took him in. "Oh really, already asking for a threesome?" she teased.

"Shut up," I hissed, as I threw the dishtowel I had been using before at her face.

"Whatever, I don't share," Seth said, leaning over the counter and kissing me.

"What are the plans?" I asked, ignoring Grace as she stuck her tongue out at me.

"Brody is racing tonight and some guys with big money will be betting. I think I am going to get in on the action," Seth said, his eyes glowing with excitement.

I felt my stomach drop as anxiety coursed through me. I didn't like the sound of anything illegal that included Seth. He had worked so hard to clean up his act, I didn't want to see him throw all of that away.

"Do you think that is a good idea?" I asked, biting my lip with worry.

Seth's smile faded and was quickly replaced with a frown. "Sure, the Raven's Brothers do it all of the time. Besides, I'm not the one racing. It's not dangerous for me," he added.

I thought about this for a moment before responding. I glanced at Grace who had a huge smile on her face telling me she was already agreeing to go.

"Fine, what time?" I asked.

"I will be at your house at eight. We need to take your car, unless Grace wants to drive separately," Seth said.

"No, we will take Mia's car," Grace chimed in. "I don't want to drive to a biker bar by myself. Who knows what those thugs might do. No offense," Grace snapped, realizing what she had just said.

Seth laughed as I slapped her arm. Even though the Raven's Boys were a gang, they were good guys. People just needed to learn more about what they stood for, before they passed judgment.

"So, you will go?" Seth asked again.

"Yes, be at my house at eight," I said, though I didn't sound too happy.

Seth smiled before placing one more kiss on my lips. "That's why I love you, Mia. You always are ready to be by my side," he said, before jumping off the bar stool.

"Where are you going?" I asked, sad to see him leave so quickly after he had arrived.

"I gotta go help Brody get his car ready for tonight. I will see you later. Love you," Seth yelled, as he rushed out of the shop.

Grace chuckled to herself. "Damn, that boy has it bad for you. I bet if you told him you wouldn't go, he wouldn't have either," she smirked.

I tried to fight the smile that grew on my face, but I couldn't. She was right; Seth loved me and he would do anything I asked. But, I couldn't be selfish.

"Now, we just need to find you a hot guy to love, too," I giggled.

"Story of my life," Grace sighed. "I just wish one day I could find a guy to look at me the way Seth looks at you," she finished.

I laughed as I got back to work. As the morning continued, I couldn't help but feel a tiny sense of dread as I thought about tonight. I just had to push those thoughts away, worrying wouldn't change the outcome, right?

# 4

*Seth*

While Mia was busy working in her brother's coffee shop, I took the afternoon to help Brody get his car prepared for the race. I knew Mia wasn't thrilled with the idea of going to the races, especially since they were held at the Raven's Boy bar, but I knew it would be good money. I hadn't told Mia yet, but I had been looking into colleges. Now, I wasn't dumb enough to ever think I could get into a big name university, but I could probably get my grades up enough to get admitted into the local community college. My goal is to get a business degree that can help me start my own custom design shop. I know I could get enough business through the Raven's Boys members and their referrals.

Now, I just had to keep myself out of trouble and my mind focused on my future.

"Dude, get your head out of your ass and help me," Brody grunted, as he stood over the engine in his car.

I shook my head to clear my head. It seemed like more times than not, my mind always drifted to Mia and the future we could possibly have one day.

"Sorry," I grumbled, as I handed him the wrench he had asked for.

Laughing, Brody just smirked as he got back to work. He had been seeing a girl lately, and ever since, he had stopped messing with me so much about being so attached to Mia. He hadn't introduced us to her yet, but I could tell it was starting to get serious.

"So, how many people do you expect to be there tonight?" I asked, trying to act nonchalant.

Still working on the car, Brody huffed. "Not really sure. Just depends on how many people get the word out. All I know is that there are going to be some big spenders there ready to bet on the races," Brody said.

I felt excitement course though me at the thought of the money I could make tonight.

"Do you even have money to bet?" Brody asked.

It sounded offensive, but I knew he was coming from a good place. He was concerned. From the stories I had heard passed around the Raven's Boy Clubhouse, some of these guys bet hundreds and thousands of dollars on the racers. We both knew I didn't have that kind of money, but I sure hoped to leave tonight with some.

# 5

## Mia

After work, I rushed home to shower before Seth and Grace showed up to get me. I had thought about the races all day and I had managed to freak myself out.

I stood underneath the warm water and allowed it to cascade down my body, rinsing away the worry and dread that had consumed me all day. The only thing keeping me sane right now was the thought of seeing Seth soon.

When I finished, I stepped out of the shower and into my closet. I selected a pair of jeans, red Converse sneakers, and a black halter top. I may not feel ready to attend these races, but at least I look the part.

Just as I finish tying my shoes, I hear the familiar roar of Seth's motorcycle. A smile spreads over my lips as I peek out my bedroom window and spot Seth parking his bike in my driveway. Isaac is at his night class, so thankfully, I don't have to explain myself tonight.

I race out of my room and down to the front door just as Seth opens it and appears inside my house.

"Hey beautiful," he says, as I jump into his arms.

He holds me as he plants a kiss to my lips, instantly taking away any worry I had once felt. "You look hot," Seth says, his eyes drinking me in.

"Thanks," I say, my cheeks blushing from the way he is looking at me. I will never get tired of the way his eyes seem to say so much.

"Do we have time?" Seth asks, winking as he insinuates going up to my room.

As much as I would love to go be alone with him, I know Grace will be here soon.

"Not now, but maybe later," I tease.

"Definitely later," Seth agrees.

Just then, we hear Grace pull up and we both groan. I slide down Seth's body, feeling every inch of his chiseled chest and arms. I can't help but feel a little guilty wishing my best friend wasn't here, but I need to just get over it.

"Mia? Seth? Grace calls out, as she opens the front door.

I quickly straighten out my clothes as she rounds the corner to where we are. A knowing look crosses her face and she smiles. "What were you all doing?" she teases.

"Nothing," I say.

"Yeah, thanks to you," Seth jabs back.

Grace just rolls her eyes and I take a moment to check out her outfit. She has on skin tight jeans, tall black boots, and a blood red tank top. I guess like me, she decided to dress for the occasion.

"Come on, we need to go or we will be late," Seth orders, as he places his hand on the small of my back.

He leads us outside and to my black Range Rover. He takes my keys and gets into the driver's seat. I sit next to him in the passenger's seat and Grace gets in the back. We make the short drive across town to where the Raven's Boys Clubhouse and bar is located. I never come over here and as the sky grows dark and I see all the wild people crowding around, I remember why.

Seth parks my car under a street light and I grow nervous. Taking my hand, he leads us into the bar where we are instantly gawked at. I mean, we are high school kids. Sure, this place is used to underage guys hanging around, but I am sure Grace and I stick out like a sore thumb.

"Seth, people are looking at us," I whisper next to him.

"Don't worry, Brody is here. Besides, these people know me," Seth says with confidence.

We continue to walk through the crowded bar until we reach the back door. A guy with dark hair nods to Seth and I recognize him as Brody. Seth has shown me pictures of them together over the years.

"Hey, you must be Mia," Brody says, offering me his hand.

I shake it and smile.

"Yes, and you must be Brody," I say.

"Yep, the one and only," he laughs.

Slapping Seth on the shoulder he grins and I notice Seth looks a bit red in the cheeks. I wonder if he talks about me to Brody?

"I'm glad you all came to watch me race. Seth has spent a lot of time helping me to get ready," Brody says.

"Yeah, well it better pay off," Seth says, and I feel my stomach drop.

I am quickly brought back down to reality that we are here so Seth can bet on the races. My anxiety begins to race and I suddenly want to be anywhere else but here.

"It will," Brody says, ignoring me freaking out next to Seth.

I hear a loud noise outside and Brody smiles. "Looks like the races are about to start," Seth says.

Brody opens the back door and everyone inside makes their way out and to a back alley. I spot two mustangs parked side by side and about a hundred more people eagerly waiting for the races to begin. To my left, a group of guys are huddled in a circle and I see a scrawny guy with blonde hair taking money as he writes something down on a small notepad.

"Wait right here and don't move," Seth orders. He walks Grace and I over to the wall of the building where a bright light is shining. "I will be right back," he says, before jogging over to the guys.

My heart is beating like a wild drum and I want to tell him not to leave, but I don't. "What is he doing?" Grace nervously asks next to me.

"Betting on the races," I say through my teeth.

We both watch as Seth talks to the scrawny guy and then hands over some money. I don't like this. Not at all.

After a few minutes, I spot Brody getting into one of the cars as Seth makes his way back over to me.

"The race is starting, come on, I want to watch," Seth says, taking my hand once again.

The night air is cool, but it does nothing to warm the fire inside of me. There are so many people watching, it is hard to get a good glimpse of the race.

"Where will they race?" I ask.

"Down the alley. The first guy to the street wins," Seth tells us.

A woman in a tight, short skit walks to the front of both vehicles as I hear engines roaring and men whistling. She lifts her hand in the air and smiles at both drivers. My heart accelerates into overdrive as I sense Seth getting nervous too. He has put money on this race and if Brody doesn't win, he will lose.

The woman drops her hands and like magic, both cars are off. A black smoke trails behind them as I watch on with a strange fascination.

# 6

## *Seth*

I throw my hands up in the air as I watch Brody race. My heart is beating like crazy and I have never been this filled with adrenaline before. I can't take my eyes off the two cars speeding down the alleyway, hoping that Brody brings me some money tonight.

I swear, it's like my heart stops beating while the cars fly past me in a blur. All I hear is screaming in my head telling me that tonight, I am going to win big.

And, I do.

As Brody crosses the finish line, I jump into the air with my arms flailing about wildly.

"Hell yeah," I scream, as I look at Mia.

She is standing there, so beautiful and strong, and all I can think about how this is all for her. I want to tell her that, but right now isn't the time.

"Did Brody win?" Mia asks, and I see Grace roll her eyes at her best friend.

"Duh, of course he won," Grace says, popping gum in her mouth. She's been watching a few of the guys who came to watch the races and I already know she is about to go saunter off to find one.

I walk over to Mia and wrap my hands around her tiny waist and pull her close to me. Her body is cool to the touch from the night air, but I know she's about to warm up when I start trailing light kisses down her neck. That always does the trick.

"Baby, I won big. Let me go collect my winnings, then we can get out of here," I say, before crashing my lips down on hers.

She moans, a slight sound escaping her lips and it is almost my undoing. I still don't know how I managed to score such an amazing girl, but I will do everything in my power to keep her.

After a minute, I release Mia and I almost laugh as she stumbles back. Damn, that is so hot how my kisses affect her that much. "Don't go anywhere," I smirk.

Mia just stands there and smiles at me while nodding her head ok. I make my way through the heavy crowd to where the guy I met earlier is standing. He's yelling at people to back up as the winners approach.

I feel a vibration coming from my pocket and pull out my phone while I wait my turn in line.

**Brody**: *Hey man, did you see my epic win?*

**Me**: *Hell yeah. You made me $1000!*

**Brody**: *Glad to help. I'm meeting some buddies at the Raven Clubhouse if you want to join me.*

**Me**: *Nah, I've got other plans*

**Brody**: *AKA Mia*

**Me**: *See you later and great race*

I laugh to myself as I stuff my phone back inside my pocket. Any other time I would have jumped at the chance to go to the Raven's Clubhouse. Hell, anything Raven I would kill to be part of. But now, my priorities have shifted a bit. Being with Mia far exceeds any want or desire to be with the Raven Boys. I guess my love for her is greater than any love I could have for that club.

I finally made my way up to the front of the line and when the guy handed me an envelope with a thick wad of cash inside, I swear I almost passed out.

He merely nods my way, then gestures for me to move on. To him, this is just another business transaction, but for me, this is a life changing moment. I've never held this much money in my hands before. It almost feels surreal.

As I turn to make my way back to Mia, I see a text from Grace.

Grace: Hey Mia and Seth. I met a new friend, he's going to give me a ride home. Don't wait for me!

I chuckle to myself as I see three little dots forming from Mia. I'm sure she's going into protective mode, but I am beyond ecstatic that Grace won't be the third wheel tonight. I have plans with Mia and only Mia.

I take a deep breath as I stuff the large wad of money in the envelope inside my jacket pocket. Then, I grab Mia and we head to the one spot in the world that is just ours.

****

Twenty-minutes later and we are nestled together on a flat spot by the pond. The moon creates a soft glow above and a light breeze adds just enough cold to make it comfortable when we cuddle together. With Mia wrapped in my arms, and money to take care of her within my pocket, I feel like I could conquer the world.

Moving a piece of loose hair out of her face, I turn and look at the beauty lying next to me. The moon lights up her face and it almost takes my breath away.

Seeing me staring at her, Mia smiles at me. "What are you doing?" she questions with a giggle in her voice.

I lean down and kiss her gently before I dare respond. Her lips were beckoning to me and I just had to get a taste. "I just can't get over how beautiful you are," I say, as I grab her hand and lace our fingers together.

She goes to look down, a habit she has when she feels embarrassed, but I stop her. "Don't look away. Own the fact that you are insanely gorgeous," I say.

"You are crazy," she laughs, but I can see on her face that my words mean a lot to her.

"Crazy about you," I tease back.

Mia curves her body into mine and it's like we become one. I wish more than anything that we could just lay like this forever.

"Hey, I have an idea," I state, not daring to move either of us right now.

"Yeah, you have a lot of ideas," she laughs.

She's right, but this one feels right. "How about you come over tomorrow and meet my mom. She has been dying to finally meet you," I add.

Mia looks up at me with wide eyes. "Seriously?" she asks, her voice rising another octave. It is cute and sexy all at once.

"Yes, I need my two favorite girls in the world to become besties," I laugh.

"Besties?" Mia mocks. "Yes, I would love to come over tomorrow. Seth Parker, you never cease to amaze me," she says, before leaning down and captures my lips with hers. She tastes so sweet and delicate and all I want to do is remember her kiss forever.

# 7

## *Mia*

I pull up outside of Seth's house and spot him instantly.

He's hunched over a metallic blue camaro, a paint gun in one hand as he carefully crafts a design. However, that is not what catches my eyes. No, it is the fact that he is dressed in only a pair of loose fitting jeans that hang low on his hips. His ripped chest sparkles in the afternoon sunlight as sweat glistens down his abs.

I lick my lips at the sight. Damn, I am so lucky to have such a hot boyfriend.

Noticing my stare, Seth smirks as he continues working. He knows that I am checking him out and he loves it.

"Maybe I should start charging for the show," he says, his cockiness on high alert.

I roll my eyes as I smile. "You would be a millionaire by Monday," I tease.

Seth laughs as he turns off the paint gun and struts over to me. Wrapping his hands around my waist, he pulls me in for a kiss. I squeal as his sweaty body rubs up against mine, but who am I kidding? I love it. I only just left him a few hours ago, but when we are apart, it feels like an eternity.

"I want to show you something," Seth says, taking my hand and leading me into his small garage.

Seth lives with just his mom and their house is modest, yet has a very warm and welcoming feel to it. A tiny pain of hurt registers in my heart as I am reminded of the very fact that Seth has yet to introduce me to his mom. I mean, we are in love and he has met my brother, but that is still a part of him that he has hidden from me.

I follow next to him and stop when Seth pulls out a small box.

"What is that?" I ask.

"I got you something," he smiles.

I take the box and open it, only to find a beautiful black diamond necklace. The diamonds are in the shape of a heart. It is absolutely perfect.

I gasp, tears stinging my eyes. "This is beautiful," I cry out.

"I bought it this morning. I took some of the money I won last night," he beams.

"I never asked, how much did you win?" I ask, staring at the beautiful gift.

Seth takes the necklace from me and places it around my neck. "Over a thousand," he says, his voice filled with excitement.

"Wow," I breathe.

"Yeah. I plan on saving most of it so I can hopefully soon put down a deposit on a building so I can start my own business after high school," he says.

"That is incredible," I say, kissing him.

Suddenly, the front door opens and a woman steps out. "Seth, are you out there?"

Seth's eyes meet mine and a glint of happiness fills him. "Come here, I want you to meet my mom," he says.

And just like that, this moment went from great to fantastic.

I follow him around to the front door and I grow nervous with every step I take. What if she doesn't like me? Do I look good enough? I'm only in jeans and a t-shirt, I didn't prepare for this.

When we stop on the small concrete porch, the woman smiles at me. She looks a lot like Seth, with dark eyes and hair. She is average height and a little bit heavier, but she has a caring smile.

"Mom, I want you to meet Mia," Seth says, smiling down at me.

His mom reaches out and pulls me in for a hug. "Oh Mia, I have heard so much about you. I am so glad Seth finally let me meet you," she says, enveloping me in a huge hug.

I revel in the moment, allowing her to comfort me in a way only moms can do. It has been so long since I have been hugged by a mom, I almost forgot how great it is.

She pulls back and looks me over. "You are even prettier than Seth described," she says.

I blush, hating the compliment but feeling proud too. "Thanks," I say.

"Mia loves my gift," Seth gushes, showing his mom my necklace.

"I'm so glad. This boy was a nervous wreck when he bought it."

I smile, not daring to tell her how he earned the money for such a beautiful gift. Instead, I just accept it and remain grateful for the moment.

Seth's mom invites us in and we spend the afternoon talking and sharing stories of our childhoods. I laugh, cry, and smile as I feel like for the first time in a very long time, that I am part of a family.

# 8

*Seth*

I walk through the halls of Hollow Cove High feeling like a new man. I've got more money in my pocket than I have ever seen before, my mom and Mia hit it off great, and for once in my life, my future is looking bright.

"Hey man, where were you yesterday?"

I turn and spot Brody running to catch up with me. I wave at him as I stop. "I spent the day with Mia and my mom and then relaxed," I say.

I knew Mia wasn't thrilled that I was betting on Brody's races, but I had plans to take her to our spot this weekend and give her a picnic dinner. I saw it in one of the cheesy movies she loves and thought it might work to cheer her up. She hadn't said she was upset, but I had read it off her body language.

"Ok, well don't forget about your meeting with a few of the guys at the Raven Boys's Clubhouse tonight," Brody reminds me.

I had been so caught up with everything else, I had almost forgotten about my biggest dream of all-- a in with the Raven's Boys. Somehow, Brody had talked me up to a few of the guys and I was going to get some pretty sweet custom orders.

"I won't miss it," I say.

Brody nods before turning and making his way to his first class of the day. I make my way into my class and pull out of my phone. I sent a quick text to Mia.

**Me**: *Hey beautiful*

I smile when she responds instantly.

**Mia**: *Hey!*
**Me**: *Don't make any plans for Saturday*
**Mia**: *Why not?*
**Me**: *I have a surprise*

**Mia**: *I don't like surprises*

I chuckle at her response. She is so sassy and stubborn.

**Me**: *Too bad*
**Mia**: *Fine, but you better make it good*
**Me**: *I always do*
**Mia**: *Love you*
**Me**: *Love you more*

I put my phone back in my pocket and tune into another boring lecture from my teacher, but all I can think about is my meeting later.

****

As soon as the last bell of the day rings, I race out of school. I hate not saying bye to Mia, but she will understand. I told her during lunch about my meeting and she was thrilled for me. I hop on my bike and drive to the other side of Hollow Cove to the Raven's Boys Clubhouse. The bar is already packed and the parking lot is filled with motorcycles of every make and kind.

I walk inside and spot Brody waiting for me at the bar. He offers a nod and begins to walk out back to the alley. The same alley where I watched Brody race just a few nights before.

I make my way out back and see a few of the other guys waiting for me. I hate that I'm nervous, but I am. This is a huge deal and they don't let just anyone work on their bikes. Getting this type of in would mean the world to me.

"Seth, these guys here are looking for someone to paint some logos on their bikes for the club. They need them done in two weeks. Is that going to be a problem?" Brody asks, his voice gruff.

"No, I can do it," I say, even though that is a ton of work for one person. But, I would be crazy to turn down any offer from them.

"Ok, you will do all the work here in Jameson's shop," Brody adds.

I nod, showing them I understand and accept. The owners of the bikes just nod too, before walking into the bar again.

"Don't mess this up," Brody says, as he slaps me on the back and then follows the guys into the bar.

I stand outside the alley alone for a few minutes. A smile creeps over my face as I realize I am one step closer to getting into the club I have waited my entire life to be part of.

# 9

## *Mia*

This week couldn't have gone any slower. I spent all week drowning in school work while Seth lived on cloud nine. He spent his evenings working on custom orders from some of the bikers in the Raven's Boys clubhouse. When we did get a chance to talk, it was all over the phone and all he could talk about was the stupid money he had won at Brody's race. I was growing more agitated by the day over his obsession with betting. I was so proud of Seth when he wanted to start his own business, now I feared he may find another passion.

As I lay on my couch, the television silently buzzing in front of me, I hear my phone go off. I scan the caller ID to see Seth's name appear. Answering, I know I sound exhausted.

"Hello?"

"Hey, is everything ok?" Seth's worried tone rings in my ears.

"Yes, sorry. I am just tired from working and school," I say, which is partly true.

"Oh, well I can't wait until tomorrow," he gushes.

This brings a real smile to my face now. Seeing Seth and getting to spend time at our spot will surely bring me out of this funk.

"Me too, I miss you," I breathe.

"I know, but the money I am earning from these custom orders on top of what your brother pays me at the coffee shop and the earnings from the races, I will be able to…" he trails off, stopping himself from finishing the rest.

"Be able to do what?" I ask, my interest piqued.

"You will just have to wait until tomorrow to find out," Seth says, and I can hear him grinning on the other end of the line.

"Fine," I say, trying to sound angry.

We talk about our day and all of the work we have had in school. When we end the call, I find myself falling asleep dreaming of being with the guy I am madly in love with tomorrow.

****

The roar of a motorcycle jump starts my heart as I race down the hallway. I'm slipping on my red Converse sneakers as I stumble my way to the front door. Isaac left early this morning to open the coffee shop and I overslept.

A chuckle makes me look up and I spot Seth grinning from ear-to-ear as he watches me look like a hot mess.

"Rough morning," he teases.

"Don't start," I grumbled.

He extends a hand and helps me finish putting on my shoe. I lean up on my tip toes and kiss him as I smile brightly.

"Are you ready?" Seth asks, still holding my hand in his.

"Yep," I say.

We make our way outside and like the gentleman he is, Seth helps me on his bike and we take off to my favorite spot in the world.

When we reach the little country road that leads to our spot, I feel my heart beating with excitement. I feel like it has been forever since we ventured to this little place, but in reality, it has only been a few days.

We immediately find a place where there are two large rocks we can lean against. The sun is shining brightly and the air is a nice seventy degrees. My phone buzzes and as I pull it out of my pocket, I see an alert on my calendar. It is a reminder that I have an upcoming appointment with Mrs. Rhonda for our now monthly sessions. I used to see her every week, but now that she and my brother Isaac feel like I am progressing, we moved them back to once a month. I have to admit, I did miss talking with her at times, but once a month is just fine considering it gives me more time to spend with the hunk I am sitting next to now.

As we sat, I finally noticed that Seth was carrying a black backpack. I eye him suspiciously as he kneels beside me.

"So, I got you some things," Seth says, with a boyish smile appearing over his face.

"Oh yeah," I ask, trying to sneak inside the bag he is unzipping.

"No, you just have to wait," Seth says, as he playfully pulls the bag away from my grasp.

I pretend to pout as I cross my arms over my chest. "Fine."

Seth begins pulling out a store bag and my eyes instantly light up. I recognize that bag. It is from the Mallory's Art Supplier store in town. I used to visit there all of the time to get my art supplies. What has Seth done?

Finally, he sits the bag in my lap. "Open it," he commands, but he looks so excited.

"Seth, you just gave me that beautiful necklace, and now more gifts?" I ask. I know he has been busy with custom orders and winnings from the races, but I don't want him spending all of his money on me. He needs to save it.

"I told you once that I don't deserve you. That you are too good for me. I now have an opportunity to give you the things you deserve, so let me," Seth says, grabbing my hands and forcing me to look at him.

My heart drops to the pit of my stomach. This isn't what I was expecting. Is this how he sees me? A materialistic girl?

I shake my head and drop his hands from mine. I take a step back from him and look at him like I don't know who he is.

"Is this how you see me?" I ask. Dropping the necklace, I act as though it is sizzling hot and just burned me.

"What's wrong? I see you as mine. As someone who deserves everything," Seth says. His eyes are wide now and it pains me to see the look on his face.

"No, this looks like you are trying to buy my love," I shout. The necklace lays on the ground between us like a huge barrier. "Where did the money come from?" I ask.

Seth opens his mouth to speak, but then quickly closes it shut. He runs a hand through his hair and I can tell he is trying to figure out what to say.

"Answer me!" I shout, this time tears streaming down my angry face.

"I can't," Seth whispers.

"What do you mean, you can't?" I cry out. "This is me, Seth."

"I know, but if I tell you everything…" he trails off.

My anger only rises and I feel as though I am about to burst. This isn't how we are supposed to be. We are in love. We are perfect. Nothing was ever supposed to get in the way of that. How could I have been so wrong?

"Then what?" I demand. I refuse to allow him to shut down on me now. After everything we have been through. The lies and scandals. The drama. He owes me the truth.

"Then you might leave me," Seth shouts, and his anger causes me to wince.

A rumble of thunder causes me to divert my eyes away from Seth and look up at the sky. Ominous gray clouds have rolled into the once clear sky. The world around me has turned dark and shifted, just like my heart.

A gasp leaves my lips and I have to hold back the urge to sob. "What have you done?" I ask.

A howling wind begins to roar around us and the leaves begin to fall from the trees. There is more than one storm brewing in these woods tonight.

Shaking his head, Seth takes a step closer to me, but I hold up my hand and stop him.

"No, you don't get to come near me right now. I need to know what you have done or else," I say.

I am not sure what I am prepared to threaten, but I know that if Seth has gotten himself into something dangerous, I just don't think I can stay with him anymore. My heart is begging and pleading for Seth to tell me that what I am thinking is wrong. I don't want to think the worst. I want so badly to be wrong-- but my mind is screaming at me to think clearly. The racing. The gambling. The money. I know what happens when you gamble around the Ravens. Sure, the Raven Brothers might not be into dirty tactics, but the guys who show up to Brody Raven's races are. I saw first-hand as Seth gambled with those guys and I see the money he is earning. I know better to believe the money is from his artwork on motorcycles. Sure, he gets paid, but not like this.

"Please, don't be like this. You are acting crazy," Seth laughs, and I see something dark in his eyes.

Where did my Seth go?

"Acting crazy?" I scream out, just as another rumble of thunder booms across the sky. "My boyfriend has more money than he ever has had, has been gambling, and now won't tell me the truth. And I am acting crazy? I can't do this anymore," I cry.

Seth takes a step back this time and something crosses his face that causes the remaining part of my heart to shatter. His drive to make more money has changed him. I don't know how I didn't see this transpiring. I guess I didn't want to see what was happening before my very own eyes. How could I? I had been so blinded by love, I hadn't seen Seth falling apart. I hadn't allowed myself to see the truth and now.... Now it was all crumbling right in front of me.

"Fine, if you can't see that what I am doing is for us, then maybe this isn't right," Seth growls. His voice is completely changed now.

I am numb now, lost in an ugly world of hatred and disbelief.

"I refuse to watch you go down this path. It's over," I say, before turning around and running. Raindrops begin to pound down on me from the sky and I can hear Seth shouting my name, but my legs refuse to stop.

Everything is wrong.

It's over.

# 10

*Seth*

"Mia!"

I shout her name, but the roar of the loud thunder seems to drown out the sound of my voice.

How could this happen to me? I thought that by gambling and earning more money, Mia would be proud of me. I did all of this for her and now she is just throwing it all away?

I love her more than anything in this world, but I can't make her see what I see. I can't make her see my vision for us.

I stand alone in the woods, in our spot, for what feels like forever. I wait, hoping she will come back. But, she never comes.

After the storm ends and the night darkness arrives, I make my way back home. I expect to find her walking alone on the road, but she's not there. It's almost like she just disappeared-- like a ghost that never truly existed.

I ride my bike back to my house and as soon as I get to my room, I check my phone.

Nothing.

No messages.

No calls.

Mia truly left me.

Now, what do I do?

# 11

*Mia*

It's been three days since I left Seth alone in the woods.

After I had run off, I had called Grace to come and get me. Of course, when she picked me up, soaking wet off the side of the road, she had a million questions for me.

But, all I could do was cry. I cried for the anger I felt. I cried for the loss of a future with Seth. I cried because it had all been a lie.

If someone truly loved you, they would tell you the truth. They wouldn't endanger themselves or someone they cared about, just for money.

Seeing me so upset, Grace stopped questioning me, but I knew that eventually she would ask me.

I had told Isaac I was sick on Monday and he agreed to let me stay home. He had been spending more time than usual at the cafe and not at home. I knew he was busy, but I couldn't help but wonder if there was something else going on too. I didn't have time to care about that though, my own life was imploding.

By Tuesday, Isaac knew I wasn't sick and was angry at me for skipping school. On Wednesday, a fed up Grace had shown up at my house and demanded answers.

"You don't get to hide away in bed," Grace shouted, as she threw my covers off of me.

I closed my eyes and tried to block out the sunlight filtering in through my bedroom window. I wasn't sure what time it was, but it must be sometime in the afternoon.

"I'm not hiding," I mumbled.

"Bullshit," Grace argued. "We have been best friends for far too long for you to lie to me now. I haven't heard from or seen Seth around here lately and now you are hiding in bed."

I sigh and sit up in bed. I realize that I can't hide anymore and I have to tell Grace what happened. So, I begin with the necklace and end with me calling her on the old road in the pouring rain.

As I talk and spill my heart out, Grace's eyes cloud over and the look on her face makes me cry even harder. She sees that Seth and I are over and the realization strikes me so hard, it is like a punch to the gut.

"Mia, I am so sorry," Grace says, hugging me tightly.

"It's ok. I guess I just don't understand how it all went wrong."

"I thought you two were perfect. That what you had was forever," Grace says, her eyes full of sadness for me and what was lost.

"I guess we were both wrong," I whisper.

We sit there together without speaking for what feels like forever. Finally, Grace stands up and places her hands on her hips. "It is time for you to get up. You have had your time to mourn the loss of your relationship. Now, you need to shower and get up and move on with your life," Grace says.

"I don't know..." I begin, but Grace stops me.

"No, you can't just stay here forever. Life didn't end. Besides, I know you, Mia. You want answers."

I almost laughed. Grace knows me too well. In the days I had spent huddled up in my bed, a million questions had been floating into my mind. And, she was right. I wanted answers. I deserved to know why this happened.

"You know what, you are right," I say standing up. "I deserve to know why Seth was willing to throw us away."

I head toward the door and stop before walking out of my bedroom. "I am going to find Seth and force him to tell me everything, even if it really is over."

****

After showering and dressing for the first time in days, I sit in Grace's car and swallow down the bile that threatens to climb up my throat. We are on our way to the Raven's Clubhouse, the only place I can think of to find Seth. We had driven past his house and his motorcycle was gone. It was almost dark now and I knew there was more than likely a race going down tonight.

Grace kept eyeing me as she drove, but she never said anything. I appreciated the peace and quiet she gave me. Even if my head was loud and chaotic.

As we pulled up to the Raven's Clubhouse, I scanned the parking lot for Seth's bike, but I couldn't find it in the sea of motorcycles. Loud noises echoed from behind the clubhouse and I knew I was right; there was a race tonight.

Jumping out of the car, I strode toward the back alley where the races were held. Grace ran to keep up with me. I was on a mission and nothing was going to stop me now.

We walked around the corner and the sight of two cars ready at the starting line made my stomach drop. Guys crowded around in a circle as they began to place their bets. Brody Raven stood by, laughing and smiling. It infuriated me.

I ran up to him and shoved him hard.

"What the hell?" he asked, as he dropped the beer he had been holding and it crashed to the pavement below.

Watching it shatter, Brody looked up at me in surprise.

"Where is Seth?" I demanded.

"Why did you shove me?" Brody asked, looking down at the broken glass on the ground.

"Answer me. Where is he?" I asked again, shoving his hard chest again.

Looking around, Brody gulped and I realized that he was nervous. "Look, maybe we should go inside and talk," Brody suggested.

I angrily shook my head, no. "We will talk here," I shouted over the noises around us. "Where is Seth?"

Sighing, Brody ran his hands through his hair before looking me in the eyes. "I don't know how to say this, but he is gone."

"What do you mean, gone?" Grace asked, finally speaking.

I couldn't believe what I was hearing. What was he talking about?

"You mean, he isn't here?" I asked.

I could feel tears burning my eyes but I refused to cry here. There were too many people around and a few were starting to notice the scene I was putting on.

"Look, I don't know how to save this, but Seth took off yesterday. Said you two were over and that he couldn't stay here anymore," Seth said.

His voice lowered and I could hear the sympathy ringing from his tone.

It was all too much. My legs trembled and I couldn't stand up any longer. I fell to the ground and struggled to catch my breath.

Grace screamed and rushed to catch me, but she was too late. I was on the pavement, unable to move as everything around me became a blur. Brody leaned down and I could see his mouth moving, but I couldn't hear a word of what he was saying.

Seth was gone.

It was all over now.

Everything was over.

# 12

*Seth*

I wasn't sure which was worse; leaving Mia or pretending like I didn't care.

After she left me that day in the woods, I picked up my phone every minute of every day, typing in her number, but never able to make the call.

I wanted to tell her that I was sorry. I wanted to tell her that I hadn't meant anything that I had said. In truth, I had never loved anyone in my life before she came alone. Sure, I loved my mom, but other than her, no one had mattered. I wasn't sure anyone would after Mia either.

I had thought I was tough and indestructible but nothing had been able to destroy me the way Mia had. I had to get out of town. I had to get away from anything and everything that reminded me of Mia.

Brody had begged me not to leave. He had listed off everything I had to lose if I left, but I left anyway.

"Want another drink?" a female voice asked.

I looked up from my phone and saw the crooked smile plastered on her face. I knew she saw me as the broken guy. That's who I had been before Mia and I guess that who I am again now. She saw in me a guy who was running away from something and who would probably be a quick and fun fuck.

"No," I said, waving her off.

She leaned over the counter, pushing her large tits into my face. I knew exactly what she wanted to offer me. As much as I knew I should just fuck this girl and try to forget about Mia, I just couldn't.

Sure, I had acted like leaving Mia was easy. That's what I needed everything to think. That's what I needed Mia to think. If she couldn't see the future I was building, then she couldn't see me. Mia had always deserved better than me. That much had always been obvious. I had thought that by gambling, I could earn enough money to start a new life. I wouldn't gamble forever. I could stop anytime I wanted, but Mia didn't need to see that.

I threw a few dollars on the counter and walked away. I stepped outside and looked around. I had no idea where I was. I had just driven until I ran out of gas. I stopped in the first small town I found. It wasn't permanent. I would go back home, but right now, I needed to free my mind of Mia. What that included, I had no idea.

# 13

*Mia*

Life before Seth had been simple.

I went to school, hung out with Grace, and had come to terms with the death of my parents.

Now, after losing Seth, I was lost. Nothing made sense anymore. I couldn't find the beauty in things like I once had been able to. Painting was no longer something I desired to do.

Isaac noticed the change in my behavior and even though I told her not to, Grace spilled the drama that went down between me and Seth. While he hated to see me broken-hearted, I think Isaac was a little relieved to see Seth gone. He had tolerated him, but something about Seth had always bothered Isaac. Was that a sign too?

"How are you doing?" Grace asked, as she stopped by my locker.

I had finally made my way back to school and was just getting through the days as best as I could. Everyone knew that Seth was gone.

I could feel their stares as they watched me walk down the halls. The pity in their eyes was almost as painful as the heartbreak itself.

"I'm fine," I said, slamming my locker door a little too loudly.

"Sure," Grace said, rolling her eyes.

"Do you need anything?" I asked, making my way down the hall.

Following close behind me, Grace began chatting. "Yeah. There is a party Friday night and I think you need to go."

"Friday is so far away, I will have to see," I said, trying to stall.

"It's Thursday, Mia. Friday is tomorrow," Grace said, grabbing my arm and stopping me. "Look, you have to start living again. You are going with me to that party. I don't care what you say. I will drag you there if I have to," she stated firmly.

How could I have gone through the entire week and not realized it. I knew I had been in a funk, but this really showed me just how low I was.

"Ok," I said. "Enough is enough. You are right, I will go," I stated.

Wrapping her arms around my shoulders, Grace pulled me in for a hug while she squealed with delight.

Laughing, I tried to pry her off of me, but she had me in a death grip. "You will not regret this, Mia," Grace cheered.

Finally getting out of her hold, I took a step back and looked at my excited best friend.

Maybe Grace was right. It was time for me to get out and live again. There was life after Seth, right?

# 14

*Mia*

"Why aren't you painting?"

Laying on the couch, I was lost in a reality show and stuffing my face with Doritos. My red Converse sneakers were strewn around the living room and I was sure I looked like a slob. Sitting up, I looked to Isaac who was leaning against the entry to the kitchen.

"What?" I asked.

Shoving off the wall, he walked over to me. "Mia, look at you," he said pointing to my chest.

Looking down, I noticed crumbs scattered all over my gray shirt. "Ok, so I am being a little messy. What does that have to do with painting?" I asked.

Shaking his head, Isaac stared at me. "You are not going to be that girl," he said, emphasizing the word girl. "You are so wrapped up in your own misery, that you are missing the life around you. Paint. Go party. Meet guys. Do something other than sit on this couch and waste your life away," he says.

Anger boils inside of me. "For your information, I am going to a party with Grace tonight," I say.

Shock flashes across his features. "Really?" he asks.

Before I can answer, our front door opens and Grace walks in like she owns the place.

"Come right in," Isaac says sarcastically.

Grace flashes him a smile before turning to me with a disgusted look on her face.

"You are not seriously dressed yet?" she asks.

"Help her," Isaac says, shaking his head before walking away.

Grace eyes me carefully and I know I am about to be lectured.

****

An hour later, I am dressed in a sleeveless black dress, silver sandals, and my hair is pulled back into a high ponytail. As Grace finishes my makeup, I sigh as I look at us in the mirror. Grace has been by my side through all of this.

"So, are you still seeing that mystery guy?" I ask.

It hit me that while I had been complaining and crying to Grace, I had also forgotten to ask her about her life. I had been selfish and I hated myself for being so stuck in my own world.

"Not really. It's complicated. I think I am going to date around," she says, adding some blush to my cheeks.

I nod, not sure if I should pry any further. Hopefully, she will meet someone soon that will treat her like a queen.

Once Grace is finished dressing me up, we leave and head to the party. Thankfully, it is a field party off one of the country roads. The football team is hosting the party and as we pull up to the field, it looks like the entire school is here. A raging fire ignites flashes of reds, oranges, and yellow into the black night. A bunch of kids stand around, talking and drinking while others dance to music being blasted through a trucks speakers.

We head over to where everyone is gathered and I stand awkwardly. Grace waves at a few people she knows, but I just stand by myself. It's no secret that I'm not popular, and I really have never taken the time to get to know many of my classmates.

A drunk guy stumbles over to me and almost knocks me over. A hand reaches out to help me, and as I turn, I lock eyes with a guy I recognize from my Biology class.

"Thanks," I say, as he helps me stand right again.

"No problem. Hey, don't we have a class together," he says. "I'm Mark."

I nod. "Yeah, Biology."

"Cool. Aren't you dating that Seth guy?" he asks, taking a sip from his beer.

I feel like I was just punched in the gut. I try to keep my face calm, but inside I am a disaster. I want to cry at the mention of Seth's name.

"Um, I was. We broke up," I say, trying to keep a smile on my face.

"Oh, that sucks. His bike was cool. But, I haven't seen him at school," Mark says.

"Yeah, I don't know," I sigh.

The conversation is uncomfortable and Mark offers a slight wave before walking away.

Looking around, I realize I need to get somewhere, anywhere, that isn't here. Walking around, I find a large tree where no one else is around. I sit down and pull my knees up to my chest. For the rest of the time we are here, I cry alone like the loser I am.

Grace: Where are you?

I see my phone light up with a text from Grace. Part of me wants to tell her I am miserable and want to go home, but the other part of me knows that Grace deserves this. It's my turn to do something for her. I scan the area and see Grace dancing with a guy from the football team. She looks happy.

**Me**: *Hey, just hanging around. Having a blast!*

I see Grace look at her phone while dancing and a wide smile spreads across her face. I refuse to break that smile. Tucking my phone away, I watch from a distance as everyone else lives their happy lives.

# 15

*Mia*

The week passed by like a blur. I went to class, work, and then back home. I was just going with the flow and not finding ways to be truly happy. I had even started painting again, though, my work was nothing like it used to be. Grace's words struck me hard the other day. I had to move forward. As much as I loved Seth and it killed me to lose him, I had to move on. My parents wouldn't want me sitting around letting life pass me by. I owed it to them, as much as myself, to get back on track.

"I will be back later tonight," Isaac said, as he grabbed his car keys from the entryway table.

"What?" I asked.

I had been lost in some reality television show and barely registered that Isaac was even around me. When I turned to look at him, I noticed that he was dressed up. I couldn't remember the last time I had seen Isaac dressed in something other than his trademark jeans and company shirt. Now, though, he looked dapper in a pair of khaki pants and a blue, button down shirt.

"Mia, I really need to know that you are going to be ok while I go out. Want me to call Grace to come over?" Isaac asked.

I shook my head, no, as I mustered a smile. I turned off the television and stood, walking over to him. "I promise I will be fine. I will call Grace if I get lonely, but you need to go out," I said, encouraging him to go out.

He seemed to relax a little as he saw me smile. "Ok good. I just know how much stress you have been under," he said.

We really hadn't talked much about Seth being gone, but we both know that I had not been myself lately.

"Where are you going?" I asked, raising my brows at him.

"Actually, I have a date," Isaac said.

Sighing, he seemed almost reluctant to tell me.

"That's great," I beamed.

"Really?" he asked, seeming surprised. "Her name is Lana and I met her at the coffee shop. It took me a while to ask her out. I didn't want to take time away from you after everything that has happened," he said.

Stepping toward him, I wanted Isaac to really hear me. Since our parents died, Isaac had given up his entire life to take care of me. It was his turn to do something for himself for once.

"Isaac, you need to focus on you. I think it's great that you have a date. Maybe I can meet her one day," I added.

"Let's just see how tonight goes," he said, reaching for the door.

"I won't wait up," I said, giggling.

Isaac walked out the door and I couldn't help but laugh.

Realizing how important it was for Isaac to go on this date, I did something I never imagined I would be doing. I ran to my bedroom and retrieved my phone. Dialing Grace's number, I waited for Grace to answer.

"Hey, what's up?" Grace asked, as soon as she answered.

"Isaac is out on a date tonight," I said. I flopped down on my bed and stared up at my ceiling as we talked. It was the first time in what felt like forever that I acted like a teenager.

"Wow, that's new," Grace laughed. "I thought he was going to become a monk or something," she teased.

"Yeah, me, too. But honestly, it's time for Isaac to get out and act like a young guy. He took on the father role and hasn't focused on himself. I am really happy for him."

"Me too. Your brother is pretty great," Grace agreed.

"Well, that is actually why I am calling," I began. "Seeing Isaac go out tonight made me realize that I can't continue to live in self-pity anymore. Seth left and made his own bad choices. Now, it's my turn to move on. I want you to set me up on a date," I finished.

"Really?" she squealed. "I thought you would never ask. I will find someone that you will just adore," Grace almost yelled into the phone.

"Thanks," I stated.

We talked for a few more minutes before finally getting off the phone. I went to bed that night feeling hopeful for the first time in what felt like forever.

# 16

*Seth*

I don't know what I had been thinking.

Telling Mia that I was leaving town was my only option. If she knew that I was still around, she never would have let me go.

Each day without her, I felt like I was dying. All I had left was a picture taken when we were still happy. I kept it in my pocket and looked at it everyday. I swear, it was the only thing that kept me going. At night, I would drive past her house when I knew she was fast asleep. Then, I would listen to her old voicemails, just so I could hear her voice again.

In my dreams, I would see her. We would go to our spot and ride on my bike together. There were times when I never wanted to wake because once morning came, Mia would leave me again.

Sitting in my backyard, I saw my phone light up with an incoming call. Answering, I knew it was Brody.

"Hey man," I said, sighing as I sat back on the medal chair.

"How are you holding up?" Brody asked.

He asked the same thing everyday. Ever since he told me about Mia showing up at the Raven's Clubhouse and losing her shit on him, I hadn't been the same.

"I'm as good as can be expected. Any updates?" I asked.

This was also part of our daily conversations. I wanted to know how Mia was, but I could never make myself say her name aloud. It hurt too much. At least in my dreams, she didn't feel real.

"She seems to be doing better I think. I even spotted her brother, Isaac, out on a date last night. Look man, I know that you think leaving Mia was best, but…"

I couldn't let him finish that statement. I knew what he was going to say; that if I just talked to Mia, I could make everything right again. But, I just couldn't do that, yet. If I could only finish paying off the warehouse and build my company I could prove to Mia that I was deserving of her love. Right now, I wasn't good for her. Honestly, I wasn't sure if I ever would be.

"Brody, you are my best friend, but I already told you, I won't talk about any of that," I seethed.

"Fine," he sighed.

"Well, I thought I would tell you there is another race happening Saturday night. From what I hear, big money is being passed around."

I nodded, even though he couldn't hear me.

"I will be there. Just do me a favor, make sure Mia doesn't show up," I said, before hanging up the phone.

Now, I just needed to tune up my bike and pray that I won this race. My entire life depended on earning the money I needed. Without it, I wouldn't be able to pay back my gambling loans or win back Mia.

# 17

*Mia*

Friday after school, I was sitting behind the counter at our coffee shop while Isaac was on another date with the same woman from the other night. I still hadn't met her yet, but I trusted his judgment and knew that if he liked her, she must be pretty great.

I heard the bell chime, and I looked up to see Grace sauntering into the shop.

"Hey," I said, waving at her.

She sat at one of the barstools at the counter and began sorting through a menu. We both knew what she was going to order, but she always did this same song and dance.

"Why don't you just go ahead and order your blueberry scone and hazelnut coffee?" I asked, rolling my eyes at her.

"Fine," she huffed, giggling a bit.

I got to work getting her order ready when I heard the bell chime again. I don't bother looking up, but when I go to hand Grace her food, her head is turned and her mouth is hanging down to the floor.

I followed her gaze to where two guys just walked in. I pause, holding her scone and coffee in mid-air as I watch them find a seat by the window facing the street.

They are both gorgeous with blonde hair and bright blue eyes.

"Wow," Grace breathes, as she slowly turns back to face me.

"Yeah," I agree, placing her coffee in front of her. I drop the scone and then shake my head.

"Those guys are really hot," Grace says, in a whisper.

"Not my typical type, but I have to agree, they are nice to look at," I add.

This gets Grace's attention. "They aren't wearing leather and riding motorcycles, so yes, they are not your type. Maybe that's a good thing," Grace states.

"What are you talking about?" I ask, grabbing a rag to wipe down the counter.

Grace takes a bite of her scone and I watch as the crumbs fall to the plate below. "Seth is what you are looking for, but I think you need to find someone who is the opposite of Seth. Think about it; you need someone safe and who won't run when things get though," Grace finishes, eyeing me carefully.

I think over her words for a minute and suddenly, I realize she is right. Maybe the best thing to do to get over Seth is to date someone unlike him. Grace takes a sip of her coffee and then moves off of the stool.

"What are you doing?" I ask, grabbing her hand as she slides off the stool.

"I'm going to get us dates," she says, winking at me.

She brushes my hand off of hers, and then walks over to the guys.She sways her hips in a suggestive manner, and the guys look up, both smiling as she approaches their table. Another waitress is already over there taking their orders, but that doesn't stop Grace from introducing herself to them. I can't hear their conversation, but I see Grace smile and laugh several times.

I try to keep myself busy at the counter, acting as though I'm not dying to know what is happening at the table. When Grace finally comes back to the counter, my heart is beating wildly in my chest.

She sits, takes a bite of her scone, and is silent.

It's killing me to not ask her what happened and she knows it.

Finally, I can't take it anymore. "Grace, tell me what you just did," I beg, glaring at her.

Grace lets out a laugh, taking a sip of her coffee before answering me. "I knew you were interested," she gloats at first. "Anyway, I told them about how we were looking for plans this weekend. They want to take us out tomorrow to the fair," she said.

The fair? In my days of self-pity, I had completely forgotten about the yearly fair that happened in Hollow Cove.

"Are you serious?" I ask.

"Of course, I'm serious. Get ready Mia, you are going to get over Seth this weekend," she says.

I lean my elbows on the counter and smile, though my heart is breaking inside at the thought of Seth not taking up my heart and mind anymore.

# 18

## *Mia*

*We sat in silence for what felt like an eternity. Every now and then Seth would plant small kisses up and down my neck, before moving up to my lips and right below my chin. I closed my eyes and drowned in the way he made me feel, it was so intoxicating.*

*"Damn, I could stay right here with you forever," Seth growled.*

*I pulled away for a moment and looked deep into his eyes. "Seth, what are we doing?" I asked.*

*Chuckling, Seth smiled. "Right now, I am tasting your sweet skin," he moaned.*

*Putting my hand on his chest, I stopped him from moving close again. If he kept this up, I would never find the courage to speak up. "No, I mean, you and me?"*

*Seth looked at me carefully before backing away. "What do you mean?" he asked, taking a nervous gulp.*

*I could feel my hands shaking as I fought to speak the next words. "Well, we have been hanging out a lot, and doing other stuff...Are we…"*

*"Are you looking for a label?" he asked. "I mean, you know I like you and I know you like me, but… I am not sure this would work outside of this place," he finished, waving his arms around indicating the field.*

My eyes shoot open and I am struggling to breathe. I had been dreaming of a time when a small misunderstanding was the biggest concern for me and Seth. The memory brings back all of the pain that I had thought was gone. Missing Seth was like taking a bullet and I wanted nothing more than to take the pain away, but even when I slept, my mind couldn't forget about him.

Glancing at my bedside clock, I noticed it was after five in the morning. I had heard Isaac come home after midnight from another date, and I had been struggling to stay asleep. I wasn't sure why I was so restless, but something told me it had something to do with my upcoming date. Realizing there was no way I was going back to sleep now, I got out of bed and got ready for the day. It was crazy, but I kept myself busy with cleaning my room and bathroom. The sun wasn't even up yet and I had managed to clean my entire house.

When Isaac came walking out of his bedroom hours later, he looked around at our sparkling clean house like he wasn't sure he was in the right home.

"Um, Mia. What's going on?" he asked, rubbing the sleep out of his eyes.

"I couldn't sleep, so I decided to clean," I said, shrugging my shoulders like it wasn't a big deal.

"Are you ok?" he asked me, as he walked into the kitchen.

I followed closely behind him and watched as he began to make a pot of coffee.

"I'm fine, Isaac. Just had a bad dream," I admitted, sitting down at the kitchen table.

Isaac made us both coffee and then joined me at the table. We sat there in silence for a few minutes before he began to speak. "Mia, I know you have been doing better, but I am still worried about you," he said, sipping his coffee.

"I know, but I promise I am working through things. In fact, Grace and I have a double date tomorrow night," I said.

I saw Isaac's eyes grow wide as he stared at me in shock. "Really?"

"Yes. Just like you said, I have to move on. Honestly, I was inspired by your decision to date again. I had to open my eyes and realize that Seth and I are over. I can't just sit around and mope all day. You and I are going to move on and get our lives back," I say, smiling at Isaac.

A bright smile spreads across his face. He looks so much younger when he smiles and is relaxed.

"Well, I'm really glad to hear that. How about I invite Lana over for dinner so you can meet her?" he asks.

"I think that would be great," I say.

Isaac and I talk a few more minutes before he rushes off to get ready for work. I spend the rest of the day painting and listening to music. Isaac and I finally are taking the necessary steps forward in getting our lives back. Now, I just needed to forget I ever met Seth.

****

Before I knew it, it was time for my double date with Grace. I still didn't know our dates names, a minor detail that Grace refused to give me. According to Grace, she was afraid that if I knew their names, I might stalk them on social media and learn too much about them. Honestly, I think she thought I was going to bail out or something. It wasn't impossible due to my behavior lately, but I was really trying now.

Grace and I drove to a small cafe where we were going to meet the guys before heading to the fair. Again, Grace had every step of this date planned. Apparently, you always went to a small location first and if you didn't like the guys, you could leave without being too far into the date. I had to give it to Grace, she knew her way around the dating game. I had been so out of the loop, I wasn't privy to these insane rules.

When we arrived at the cafe, we spotted the guys waiting outside for us. As I got out of the car, I took a few extra seconds to really get a good look at the guy who was my date for the evening. He had shaggy blonde hair, blue eyes, and was dressed very nice in khaki shorts and a light blue Polo shirt. He was presentable and seemed like a true gentleman. I couldn't help the stabbing pain in my heart as I realized he was the complete opposite of Seth. Maybe that was why Grade had chosen him.

Following Grace, we greeted the guys and made our way inside of the cafe.

"Hey," my date said. He extended his hand out to me. "So, apparently we weren't supposed to know one another's names," he said, almost laughing.

I was glad that he was making light of the situation. It made me feel a little bit better. "Yeah, my friend Grace is a little nuts. Anyway, I'm Mia," I said, taking his hand and shaking it.

"Hey, Mia. I'm Alex," he said.

I waited for the sparks to fly or electricity to pop, but nothing happened.

Disappointment filled me and I tried to hide it from showing on my face. Alex and I followed Grace, and her date, Aaron, to a small table facing the street. We each ordered frappuccinos and chatted about our schools--they went to the school across town-- and our jobs. The guys were friendly enough, but there was something missing.

Just as Alex turned to ask me a question, the roar of a motorcycle filtered inside the cafe and I swear, I felt my heart stop. Sitting up straighter, I pressed my face against the window and stared out to the street. Two older guys pulled up to the stoplight and let their bikes go idle for a minute. Realizing it wasn't Seth, I sat back and my body relaxed. As I looked up again, I spotted Alex and Aaron looking at me like I had lost my mind and Grace was staring daggers at me.

Great, I knew I would hear about that later.

"So, I guess we should get going to the fair," Aaron suggested, as we were all almost finished with our drinks.

"Sure," I said.

We paid and left a tip on the table for our waitress. As we walked out to our cars, Grace grabbed my arm and stopped me.

"What the hell was that back there?" she asked, clearly meaning my insane window moment.

Shaking my head, I took a deep breath. "Nothing. I thought I saw something, but I was wrong," I said.

"I know what you thought you saw. Mia, you have to let go of Seth. He's gone and these guys are here, right here in front of us."

She was right. But, it still killed me to know that Seth wasn't coming back. I got into the car and as we followed the guys to the fairgrounds, I tried to hide the lone tear that slipped down my cheek.

# 19

*Seth*

It's too late to apologize. It's too late to beg for forgiveness. It's too late to get back everything I lost.

I know all of that now, but it still hurts like hell to know that Mia isn't mine anymore. She will always hold my heart, but she deserves better than me right now. I don't know if I will ever be good enough for her.

Leaning over the engine of a car I'm working on, I hear Brody walk up behind me. His biker boots are loud and scrape against the concrete.

"Hey man," I say, not even looking up.

Since I returned home, I have been hiding out. Anytime I need to work on a car or bike, I make sure to work at the clients house or garage. I can't risk Mia seeing me at my house, if she would ever happen to drive by. I doubt she would, but still.

Even when I race, I make sure to use a different name and wait until the last minute to get there. It's like I'm a ghost now.

Brody walks up to me and I hear him sigh. I can tell from his stance that something is wrong. Standing up, I wipe my hands on my jeans as I turn to face him.

"What?" I ask.

"Seth, the race coming up, the guys who you owe money to will be there," he said, his eyes focused on mine.

Shit. I almost have the money I owe for the bet I lost, but I still am short a couple hundred of dollars. I know these guys don't want to hear about my issues nor do they care. Running my hand through my messy hair, I stare up at the sky for a minute. I try not to panic, but I know I have gotten myself into some deep shit right now.

"I'll have it," I lie.

"Seth, are you sure?" Brody asks, narrowing his gaze on me.

We have been friends since we were kids. Brody knows me better than anyone else in the world. And right now, my best friend knows that I am lying to him. I am busting my ass to come up with the money, but around here, money isn't always easy to come by.

"Yeah, I will figure something out," I say.

"I don't like the way that sounds," Brody sighs. "Look, this whole mess started because I let you start racing behind the Raven's Bar and I introduced you to the guys who were gambling on the races. This is all my fault," Brody states.

Anger washes over me. This is not his fault. "Brody, I made the decision to race and I made the decision to get involved with those guys. If anyone is at fault here, it's me. I know that. I won't let you feel bad about any of this," I say.

Brody nods his head toward the grass and I follow as he walks over and sits under a large tree.

"How did you know where I was?" I asked.

"You told me last week you would be working on a car over here at Mark's brothers house," Brody reminds me.

Damn, my mind has gone to hell lately. I can't remember anything. Well, that's not true. I remember everything about Mia. The way her sweet voice said my name, her scent, and the way just looking at her would drive me wild. That's all I remember now.

"Oh yeah, I forgot," I say.

We sit there for a few minutes and I relax. I have been working non-stop and my body is aching.

"So, what about the warehouse?" Brody asks.

This all started because I wanted to buy a warehouse to start my own business. Now, I feel like that dream is slipping away like everything else in my life.

I run my hand over my face as I struggle to find the right words to say. "I have no idea. Everything is so fucked up right now. I feel like I'm drowning. I owe so much, I may never get that warehouse," I admit.

"I think you are putting way too much pressure on yourself. The warehouse was a dream you had because of…" he stops himself before saying her name.

I might be able to say it in my head, but hearing her name aloud is just too painful.

I nod, showing him I know what he was about to say and that I am grateful that he stopped himself.

"Well, that dream has died. All I can do now is get myself out of his dilemma, first," I sigh.

Brody pats me on the shoulder and we just sit for a few minutes longer.

"You hungry?" I ask.

"Starving. Let's go get something to eat and then I will come back and help you finish up this car," Brody offers.

"I can't ask you to do that," I begin to argue.

"You didn't. I'm offering," he says, standing up and offering me his hand to help me up.

I might be alone right now, but at least I have my best friend by my side. Honestly, he may be the only one by my side.

# 20

*Seth*

We ride out to a small burger joint just on the outskirts of town. The sun has set and the night sky is cool and feels good against my tired skin. We park our bikes and take our food over to a picnic table that faces the road.

We watch as cars pass by, all heading out to the county fair. I bite into my burger and almost moan out loud. Now that I think about it, this is the first time I've eaten all day. I have been so caught up in working, I guess I forget to eat.

I see a familiar car pull up near us and I feel like I am going to puke. A familiar head of blonde hair fills my vision and I know it is Grace, Mia's best friend.

Grace is talking and all I can see is the side of her face.

My eyes instantly travel to the passenger side of the car and as much as I know I shouldn't, I can't seem to take my eyes off the car. From where I am sitting, I can't see the passenger yet. I wait for a glimpse of that delicious chocolate brown hair.

Brody notices me staring and his eyes travel to where I am looking. I see him shake his head as a look of panic crosses his features.

I haven't seen Mia since the day she left me. I don't know if I can do this.

"Maybe we should just go," Brody offers, standing.

I'm frozen in place and unable to react or respond. It's like I can't function until I see her. Maybe just a glimpse will suffice for a while.

Grace pulls her car up a bit, the line is now extending far down the road as people wait to get onto the fairgrounds. Her window is slightly open and the light sound of music rolls out. I can hear Grace's voice and I just wait, my heart refusing to beat as I wait.

Then, I hear it.

That sultry laugh that could make me smile every time. My heart feels like it is going to explode as I finally get a glimpse of the girl who shattered my heart, but still holds all of the pieces.

Then, I see her face. That beautiful face that still haunts my mind every damn day.

"Seth, come on. Let's just go," Brody says again, this time he grabs his helmet off the table.

"No, I just need to look at her," I say, my voice barely above a whisper.

"Don't do this to yourself," Brody says, and I hear the concern in his voice.

Mia throws her head back as she slumps down in the seat. Something about her movements causes alarm in me. If I didn't know better, she almost looks upset. I lean over, placing my hands on my knees as I watch her. She's smiling, but that normal glow that usually radiates around her is gone. Her emerald green eyes seem darker for some reason and a part of me wants to run over to the car and beg her to tell me what's wrong.

But, I don't. Because I can't.

She's not mine anymore.

I see Mia sigh and she turns and that's when it happens.

It's like the earth and sun collide as everything around me shatters.

Mia sees me and our eyes lock. I feel like I have just been punched in the gut as her face stares at me. But, the worst part is the way her smile fades and tears fill her eyes. Even from the distance between us, I see the pain in her features.

I can't move. I hear Brody saying something to me, but I can't make out his words. It's like I am locked inside of a wind tunnel and I am about to lose my life.

The car moves forward as the traffic begins to move and she's gone. Almost like she was never there to begin with. But, she was.

The excruciating pain I feel right now proves that Mia was there right there in front of me and she was sad. Did I cause that pain? Did someone else hurt her? I realized right then that I had to know if Mia was ok.

# 21

*Mia*

I feel like I just saw a ghost. Was my mind playing tricks on me or was Seth really sitting on a picnic table staring at me?

My blood goes cold as I try to clear my mind. I can't tell Grace that I just saw the boy who I had fallen madly in love with, but had let walk away. If she knew, she would push harder for me to date any and every guy she encountered. I just needed to get through tonight and then tomorrow, I could find a way to know if Seth, was in fact, home.

For right now, I need to play the role of single girl. Soon enough I would get my answers.

We got out of our car and met the guys at the ticket booth. Like true gentlemen, they paid our way into the fair. Alex walked beside me while Grace and her date walked ahead of us. I knew what was going on right now, it was a classic move. Somehow, Alex and I ended up alone and I had no idea where Grace had gone off too.

"I think we lost our friends," I said to Alex.

He chuckled. "I think you are right."

"Do you like the Ferris Wheel?" he asked.

I looked up and saw the bright neon green lights of the large Ferris Wheel. It was towering above us and might be a nice way to just sit and think.

"Sure," I said, shrugging my shoulders.

Alex was a nice guy and he didn't deserve for me to act any certain way toward him. It wasn't his fault I saw a ghost from my not so long ago past. It also wasn't his fault that my heart would probably always long for Seth. Regardless if that was right or wrong.

We walked over to the Ferris Wheel and stood in line. Alex was nice and asked me questions about school and work. It was a nice conversation, but there was no spark.

When it was finally our turn, Alex helped me onto the car and we sat back as the ride began to move. As we began to move higher up, I felt a wave of anxious energy wash over me. Something in my mind told me to look around. As I began to gaze out over the fairgrounds, I saw a familiar dark head of hair. I leaned forward, forgetting that I was sitting high in the air.

Alex grabbed my hand, pulling me back before I toppled our car over and sending us flying to the ground below. "Hey, are you alright?" he asked.

I unlocked my eyes from the figure and looked over at Alex. "Yes. Sorry, I was just looking around," I said.

He seemed to accept my response and he continued to look around. I realized too, that his hand was still holding mine. I didn't want to pull away and make the rider any more awkward than I already had, so I just went with it.

My eyes traveled back to the ground and I couldn't help but wonder if my eyes and head were playing tricks on me. Then, like a punch to the gut, I saw him.

Seth.

He was standing beside the funnel cake cart and he was staring up at me.

At us.

An angry scowl masked his face and hurt reflected in his dark eyes. I closed my eyes for a minute and then reopened them. When I looked again, Seth was still standing there watching me.

Tears burned at my eyes and my heart began to beat so fast, I feared I would have a heart attack. Right then, being in this car with Alex seemed very, very wrong. His hand on mine was like a burning flame and I had to remove myself or I would get burned. I carefully slid my hand out of Alex's grasp, my eyes never leaving Seth.

I spotted Brody standing next to him, speaking something in his ear. However, Seth's gaze never wavered away from mine. Why was he here? Why was he doing this? Was this his way of hurting me? This tormenting game we were both playing was going to be the death of me.

Sensing my frigid mood, Alex cleared his throat. "Who is the guy?" he asked.

Startled, I unlocked my gaze for a moment to look over at Alex.

"What?" I asked.

He smiled and I saw that he was let down. My heart filled with guilt and I felt like a terrible person. "It's ok. I saw the way you reacted when you just saw that guy. And, I can tell that you are clearly into someone else," he said.

He was right, but it still didn't make any of this any better.

Sighing, I continued to stare at Seth and I smiled. "Alex, you are such a great guy. That guy is my ex-boyfriend and my first love. I honestly don't know what went wrong with us, but when I broke up with him, it broke me, too. I haven't seen him in a long time, well until today."

Alex nodded and placed his hand on mine. Not in a romantic way, but in a friendly manner instead. "I totally get it. Honestly, I'm still hung up on my ex-girlfriend, too. I only agreed to this date because my friend begged me and you are hot," he said.

I giggled at that and was grateful that Alex could understand what I was going through.

"Looks like we are just two very messed up people," I said.

"You said it," Alex chuckled.

I sat back in the car, and began to calm my breathing. A slight breeze filtered through the air and I realized I had been sweating. The cool air chilled my skin, but it did nothing for my racing heart.

"So, why don't you go talk to that guy?" Alex asked me.

It was the million dollar question. And, I didn't have an answer for it. Talking to Seth wouldn't be easy. There were so many emotions swirling around and we both had hot tempers.

Sighing, I smiled. "Seth and I are like fire and ice. We loved hard and fought harder. I don't know if we could talk," I said.

My heart felt like it was shattering all over again as I admitted that fact.

"I get it, but can I be blunt?" Alex asked. I nodded, letting him know to continue. "I think you and this guy need to just get everything out into the open. That's what I did. My ex and I realized breaking up was best for us, but we still talk. Maybe one day we can get back together, but it's a nice feeling to not hate her anymore," he finished.

Alex had great advice and I knew he was right, I just wasn't sure if I was brave enough to take that leap. I wasn't so sure I could trust myself around Seth. Seeing him brought up old memories and feelings that I knew would never go away.

"Maybe," I said.

The ride continued and Seth got lost in the sea of people below me. When the ride was over, I almost jumped out of the car before the guy working the ride could help me out.

I raced to the funnel cake cart where I had seen Seth, but he was gone. I felt like dropping to my knees right then and there. I had been so close to him, but yet, so far away.

"Sorry you missed him," Alex said, catching up with me.

"It's ok. I think it was probably for the best," I said, even though I didn't feel that way at all.

The sweet and grease filled air made my mouth water and all of a sudden, I wanted a funnel cake.

"This sounds insane, but I think I want a funnel cake," I said to Alex.

Chuckling, he walked up to the counter. "You read my mind. I think after our serious talk, we need some greasy food," he said.

As we ordered our food, Grace and Aaron walked up to us. Seeing her, I narrowed my eyes and glared at her, but Grade just ignored me and smirked.

"What have you two been up to?" Grace asked us, winking.

Alex and I looked at one another, before he responded. "We just rode the Ferris Wheel and now we are getting a funnel cake," he said.

I was grateful that he kept our freak-out moment our little secret. Alex was a great guy and one day, he would make some very lucky girl happy, but that girl just wasn't me.

"Awesome, I love funnel cake," Grace cheered.

We all stood around, eating our funnel cake, and watching the sights and sounds of the fair. I never told Grace about seeing Seth. I was just going to keep that as my own little secret.

# 22

*Seth*

"Slow down," Brody yelled after me.

I couldn't slow down. I kept walking faster and faster until I was sprinting to the parking lot.

Seeing Mia sitting next to that preppy looking kid was my ultimate undoing. My heart shattered again and this time, I was certain it would never be mended again.

"Just leave me alone, Brody," I shouted behind me.

I needed to be alone. I didn't want anyone seeing me right now. I was steaming hot angry and I knew it was only a matter of time before I blew up like a ticking time bomb.

"I'm not going to leave you alone, man. Just slow down and we can talk about this," Brody yelled.

He was a persistent little shit. I knew in my heart he wouldn't leave me alone. When I reached my bike, I jumped on and reached for my keys, but they weren't in my pocket.

"Fuck!" I yelled into the air.

Brody finally reached up to me as I was petting my pockets in a haste. If I had dropped them, there was no telling where they could be.

Huffing and puffing, I was walking around the bike, searching through the lot for my keys.

"Looking for these?" Brody asked, dangling my keys in front of him.

"You took them?" I asked, confused and pissed.

"I swiped them when you were standing like a zombie and watching Mia. You are in no shape to drive right now," he said, his eyes narrowed in on me.

I blew out a heavy breath and placed my hands on the back of my hair. Pulling at my hair, I screamed out again. I was losing my mind and there wasn't anything that could fix me. Well, there was one thing, but she was clearly moving on.

"Brody, I will calm down. But right now, I just need to get the hell out of here," I said, my voice hoarse from screaming.

Brody took a brave step toward me and with his other hand, patted me on the back. "Look, it's time for you to either talk to Mia or move on. But, what you are doing isn't healthy. She clearly knows you are back in town now, so just stop the disappearing act," he stated.

I wanted to punch my best friend, but I told myself not to. I knew Brody was right, but I just couldn't imagine moving on and finding anyone else. Mia stole my heart and no other woman would ever have it.

"I can't live without her," I said, finally crumbling to my knees. I fell back and landed on my ass. Pulling my knees up to my chest, I sat there, wrecked and broken.

Brody sat down next to me and just sat with me. Neither of us spoke again, we just sat alone in the parking lot while I tried to understand how my life became such a fucked up mess.

# 23

*Mia*

Ever since I saw Seth at the fair, I couldn't help but look for him everywhere I went.

On my way to school.

To the grocery.

Even when I was in class, I would catch myself glancing out the window at the street, desperately hoping for a glimpse of his dark hair on his bike. But, it was like he was never there at all. There hadn't been any more signs of Seth and I was driving myself crazy each time I looked for him.

A full week had passed and Isaac was preparing me to meet his new girlfriend, Lana. Things between them were getting pretty serious and I had never seen him more nervous in my life. It was Friday evening and Isaac had made his famous lasagna that I adored. It was a recipe my mom had taught us when we were kids. Every time Isaac made the dish, it reminded us of our childhood. I loved that he decided to make it today.

He was busy scurrying around the kitchen when I walked into the house from work. I had agreed to work an extra shift at the cafe so that he could come home early and prepare.

"Do you need any help?" I asked, looking around at the kitchen.

The table was set with four plates and four glasses. I looked over at Isaac as he pulled the lasagna out of the oven. The house smelled divine, but I was more focused on the additional plate. Had I asked Grace to come over and forgotten? It was possible. I had been so wrecked all week that anything was possible at this point.

"Hey, why are there four plates?" I ask.

If I did ask Grace, she must have forgotten too, because she hadn't said a word about it to me.

"Oh, I forgot to tell you. Lana will be bringing her niece with her. She just got custody of her and doesn't want to leave her alone," Isaac said, bringing the dish over to the table.

He carefully placed the hot tray on the pot holders in the center of the table.

"Custody?" I asked.

How old was Lana?

"Yeah. I didn't really ask a lot of questions, but apparently her older sister is a drug addict. She lost custody of the girl and Lana was the only one willing to take her in," Isaac finished.

In my head, I imagined a young child, scared and helpless. My heart broke for her. "That's terrible. But, it's great of Lana to step up. I can't wait to meet her. I will check and see if I have any old crayons for the girl to play with," I said, rushing back to my room.

I heard Isaac yell for me, but I ignored him. I had just found an old box of metallic Crayola crayons when the doorbell rang. I pulled a couple of white printer paper out of my printer and began sprinting back toward the kitchen. I reached the end of the hall just as Isaac opened the front door.

Standing in my doorway, was a beautiful woman in her twenties. Her long, red hair was styled in those amazing beach wave curls. Her blue eyes shined brightly as she looked up at my brother. I couldn't help but sigh watching them. However, my moment of sweetness was brought to an abrupt halt when I spotted the niece. Instead of a young little girl, I saw a teenager with dyed black hair, black lipstick, and fishnet stockings.

What the hell?

"Come in," Isaac said, taking Lana in and giving her a kiss.

The girl beside Lana cringed and rolled her eyes at the sentiment. They walked inside and Isaac closed the door behind them. I realized that I was standing in the middle of the hall with crayons and paper sticking out of my arms. They must think I am crazy.

"Lana, this is my sister, Mia," Isaac introduced us.

"Hi," I said, sheepishly. I felt awkward standing there. "Um, Isaac said Lana was bringing her niece," I added, noting the paper and crayons.

Lana let out a sweet laugh. "Oh my gosh, Isaac. Did you not tell her old Jamie was?" she asked, turning to Isaac.

Isaac gave me a glare before turning back and smiling at Lana again. "I tried, but Mia is stubborn and doesn't listen," he added.

I stuck my tongue out at him and everyone laughed. Well, everyone except Jamie.

"Dinner smells amazing," Lana said, breaking the awkward silence now filling the room.

"Oh yes, I just took it out of the oven. I have garlic bread, too. Plus, I bought that wine you liked from that little restaurant we went to," Isaac adds.

I'm beyond flabbergasted at the man now standing before me. My annoying older brother has been replaced with a caring and sweet gentleman. It struck me right then and there that Isaac would someday get married and create his own family. Right now, he was the only family I had. Would that change if he and Lana got married? I felt my stomach drop thinking about it.

We all walked into the kitchen and sat at the table. Isaac finished bringing over the salad and garlic bread. He poured himself and Lana some white wine while I brought Jamie and myself some ice water.

We all began eating and everyone agreed the food was delicious. Lana and Isaac chatted away while Jamie and I sat there in silence. She seemed distant and I didn't want to push her to talk if she was uncomfortable.

"Jamie will be attending Hollow Cove High starting next week," Lana said, smiling over at us.

"Really?" I asked. "What grade?"

Lana waited a minute, clearly wanting Jamie to talk, but once it was clear she was going to remain mute, Lana spoke for her. "Yes, she will be a senior."

"Mia can show her around," Isaac offered.

I almost choked on my bite of garlic bread as Isaac offered for me to play tour guide to Lana's niece.

"Sure, if I'm not too busy," I say, swallowing my food.

Isaac laughed at that. "Busy? With what? Mia and her boyfriend broke up recently and she hasn't had much to do lately," Isaac said.

I saw Lana's head spin around to look over at Isaac. While this was my first time meeting Lana, there was also an unspoken girl code that you just didn't bring up painful breakups. A mom or another woman would know this, not an insensitive brother.

"Isaac," Lana said, trying to diffuse the situation.

"No, he's right. The first guy I cared about and made me feel alive since my parents died broke my heart. So yes, I am a loser with nothing going on. Excuse me," I said, scooting my chair out before I ran out of the room. I sprinted to the front door and couldn't get outside fast enough.

I heard Isaac call after me, but I just couldn't stop. Once outside, I sighed and released a breath I hadn't realized I was holding. Tears sprang from my eyes as I walked over and sat on the curb. I extended my legs out onto the street and lay back into the cool grass. My eyes traveled up to the stars and I watched them, trying to locate the Big Dipper.

I could hear the front door open and close and my anger began to rise again. "Go away, Isaac," I said through gritted teeth.

"It's not Isaac," a voice said.

I sat up and spun around. Jamie was walking over to me. She didn't smile or say anything else, but she sat down next to me. Confused, I watched her carefully for a minute.

"I don't think he realized that what he said was mean," she offered, staring up at the stars.

I lay back down and crossed my arms across my chest. "Maybe not. It's been a rough couple of months," I admitted.

Jamie chuckled. "Tell me about it."

Oh, shit. Jamie was just taken from her mom. I was sure her life was way more messed up than mine, but I was the one being dramatic.

"I'm sorry," I said, turning my head to the side to face her.

"Don't worry about it. It's for the best, my mom is a mess," she said, her face still stoic.

"My life is a mess right now. I broke up with Seth, that was my boyfriend. He did something stupid and I just needed a break, but now…" I couldn't finish my sentence, it was just too painful.

"I get it. I had to break up with a guy I had been seeing since middle school. He was my safe place when my mom would get too high to function. Life sucks sometimes," she finished.

I had never been more grateful to have someone to share in my misery. As much as I loved Grace, she just couldn't understand the pain I felt losing my parents and then Seth. But with Jamie, it was like she understood and didn't judge me.

I didn't know this girl, but for some reason, I was sharing my life with her. And in return, she was sharing hers with me.

"So, your aunt and my brother are pretty serious," I said, changing the subject.

A slight smile appeared over Jamie's dark face. "Maybe. I know that she has spent most of her life fixing all of the messes my mom has made. She deserves to be happy and for what it's worth, your brother seems like a good guy."

I hated to admit it, but she was right. "Yeah, he drives me insane, but he didn't hesitate to take me in when our parents died. He's the only family I have."

We lay there for a little while longer in silence. It was nice laying under the stars. I heard the front door open again and this time, I heard Lana's voice.

"Girls," she called.

Jamie and I both sat up and she looked startled to see us laying in the grass beside the street. "We are out here," Jamie says.

"I came out to check on both of you," Lana said, smiling down at both of us.

"I'm fine," I say.

"We just needed to talk," Jamie stated.

Lana nodded and surprised both of us when she sat down beside us. She turned to me and I saw kindness in her eyes. "Mia, I hope I am not overstepping my boundaries here, but Isaac feels really bad," she said, offering a smile.

"Yeah, he should," I said, with a little more force than I intended.

"Breakups are tough and most boys, especially brothers, don't always understand that. I explained it to him and he honestly feels terrible. Later, when you both cool down, you should talk to him," Lana finished.

"Yeah, I will," I agreed.

Lana sat with us for a few more minutes until our buts became numb. We all three stood and began making our way back into the house. Right before we stepped inside, I stopped and grabbed Jamie's hand.

"Hey, let me know when you want that tour," I offered, smiling.

Jamie didn't smile, but a slight grin spread over her black lips. I would take that as a yes.

Feeling better, I stepped inside my house just as the faint roar of a motorcycle engine sounded somewhere in the distance.

# 24

*Seth*

My life is spiraling out of control. I feel like at one point, I had everything I ever wanted. Mia, acceptance, and I was on my way to securing a warehouse to start my own business. Now, I am going backward. All because of a few stupid mistakes.

After Brody and I had left the fair, I had gone home and talked to my mom. I knew I needed to get back to school. I couldn't stay away forever. I also needed to get the money together so I could pay off my debts. I wanted away from this life of crime I had found myself in.

Now, as I work on the hood of a custom 1969 Mustang, I allow my thoughts to keep me company. Well, that is until I hear the sounds of footsteps coming my way. I had decided to work on this new client's car at my house. He lived in a wealthy, gated neighborhood and I would stick out like a sore thumb.

"Hey, Brody," I called, assuming it was him.

Brody had been glued to my side practically everyday. I knew he was worried about me. Hell, I was worried about me, too. But, today, I hadn't seen him yet.

"Sorry, man. It's not Brody," I heard from behind me.

The hairs on the back of my neck stood as that voice resonated fear inside of me. I knew that voice. Spinning around, I came face-to-face with the guys who I had met behind the Raven's bar. The very guys who had conned me into betting on some races. And, the guys who I now owe several hundred dollars to.

"Hey, guys," I said, trying to sound nonchalant. I hoped they didn't hear the fear in my voice.

"We didn't come here to shoot the shit with you, kid," one of the guys sneers.

They had given me names once before, but I knew it wasn't their real names. I mean, what criminals offer out their true identities?

I nod, because we all know exactly why they are here. They want to collect on the money owed to them.

"I know," I say. "I have most of your money," I offer.

One of the guys steps toward me and I reflectively take a step back. My legs hit the car I'm working on and I know I am cornered.

"We don't want some of the money. We came here to collect it all," the guy sneers.

"Well, I don't have it all," I say, my tone sharp.

The guy turns for a brief second to look back at his friends, before he swings back around and punches me in the eye. I feel the sting and my hands go up to shield my face. I can hear the other guys advancing toward me and I try to run, but it's no use. They pin me down and begin punching and kicking me. Pain radiates throughout my entire body as I struggle to breathe. I go to scream, but then think better of it. These guys came here to get their money or to kick my ass. Since I don't have the money, I have no other choice but then to take the beating. I feel one last swift kick to the stomach and then the world around me goes black.

****

"Seth, can you hear me?"

A voice is calling to me, but my head is throbbing so bad, I can barely register the sound. I feel a hand on my arm, but the pain is so severe, it takes my breath away.

"Shit man, what have you gotten yourself into?" I hear the voice again.

"Brody?" I whisper, my voice hoarse.

"Yeah, Seth. It's me. What happened?" he asks.

I try to open my eyes, but one is completely sealed shut. Brody's face is nothing more than a blur right now.

"I got my ass kicked," I say, the taste of blood now filling my mouth. I spit onto the ground and even that hurts.

Brody slowly lifts me off the ground and helps me to sit. "Dude, I need to get you to the hospital. You might have broken ribs," he says.

"No," I try to argue, but it's no use. I can already feel Brody lifting me. For such a small guy, he has no issue carrying me. I try to hold on a little longer, but the pain is just too painful. I black out again and enjoy the peace for once.

# 25

*Mia*

Ever since the dinner, Lana and Jamie had become permanent fixtures around my house. Jamie started attending Hollow Cove High that following Monday and I made sure to show her around. It's not like I had a lot of friends to introduce her to. And, I think that made her like me even more. Jamie wasn't the type of girl who wanted to be part of the popular crowd. Like me and Grace, she had been picked on and enjoyed having a small circle. In fact, Jamie appeared more gothic than any other style. She preferred to wear only black and Lana seemed cool with that.

I was more than relieved when Grace and Jamie hit it off. None of us honestly had that much in common, but somehow, we all clicked anyway.

Walking into lunch, I spotted Jamie and Grace at a table by a large window. I made my way over to them and sat down. Just as I went to open my bag to retrieve my lunch, I felt my phone vibrate in my pocket. Pulling it out, I saw a number that I didn't recognize.

"Hello?" I answered, sounding weary for a moment.

"Mia?" the voice on the other end asked.

"Yes, who is this?"

"Mia, it's Brody, Seth's friend," he said.

I felt my blood turn to ice and my heart stopped. Noticing my change in demeanor, Grace and Jamie stared at me with blank faces.

"What do you want, Brody?" I snapped.

Brody was always with Seth and he was with Seth the night I spotted them at the fair. I wasn't sure what it was he could possibly want or why he would be calling me. At the mention of his name, Grace's eyes grew wide as saucers.

Jamie looked to Grace for clarification and I could hear Grace begin to fill her in.

"Mia, I know I am one of the last people you want to hear from, but I didn't have a choice. Seth is hurt," he said.

I felt like my world stopped spinning. Seth was hurt. Fear engulfed me and my arms began to shake as terrible images began to play in my mind.

"What's wrong?" I asked frantically.

"Those guys who he got the money from, they came looking for their payout and Seth didn't have it. They beat him up pretty bad. He's at Hollow Cove Hospital," Brody said.

I stood, knocking my chair over with a loud thud. A few heads turned my way, but I didn't care.

"I will be right there," I said. "Text me his room number," I shouted before hanging up.

Grace and Jamie stood, too. "What's going on?" Grace asked, reaching for my hand.

Tears poured down my face as I stared back at her. "Seth is hurt. He's in the hospital. I have to go see him," I said.

Grace nodded. "We are coming with you," she said.

We began to leave the cafeteria and rushed out the front doors. I didn't care who saw me or how much trouble I might get into for skipping the rest of my classes. Seth was hurt and I had to go to him.

****

We arrived at the hospital in less than ten minutes. None of us spoke the entire car ride. All I could think about was Seth and the trouble he had found himself in. I knew it was stupid of me to jump and rush to his side, but what choice did I have? Seth would always hold my heart. Regardless if we were together or not, I had to know that he was going to be ok.

Grace barely put her car in park before I opened the passenger door and jumped out. I ran into the hospital and bypassed the elevator. Taking the stairs two at a time, I made it to the second floor where Seth's room was located. Brody had texted me Seth's room number, 217, which was on the second floor. As I ran, I could hear Jamie and Grace yelling for me to wait for them, but nothing was going to stop me.

When I spotted Seth's room, I stopped and froze in the doorway.

Laying lifeless in a large hospital bed, Seth was hooked up to several beeping machines. Brody sat in a chair beside his bed, flipping through a motorcycle magazine. Sensing my presence, Brody looked up and locked eyes with me.

"Hey," he said, standing and closing the distance between us.

"How is he?" I asked.

Sighing, Brody ran a hand through his hair. "He has two broken ribs, a bruised collarbone, and lots of cuts and bruises. He will be ok, but Mia, Seth is in some big trouble."

I could see the worry on Brody's face and I knew how much he cared for his friend.

"Why did you call me?" I asked, stepping into the room. I walked over and stood next to Seth. From the slow rise and fall of his chest, I could tell he was sleeping. I was sure they had given him some pretty heavy pain killers that would knock him out.

Brody walked over beside me. "Mia, Seth can't get over you. He got himself into this mess because he wanted to earn the money to create a future for you all. Now, he's in way over his head. I know you still love him. I saw the way you two looked at one another the night of the fair. You needed to know," Brody finished.

He was right. About all of it. But, it still pained me to know what Seth and I needed one another this badly.

"I don't know where we go from here," I whisper.

"I don't either," Brody says.

Grace and Jamie walk into the room and I hear Grace gasp. "Is he ok?" she asks.

Brody turns and goes to fill them in on Seth's condition. All I can do is stand there and stare at Seth. He looks so peaceful right now, but I now know, it's all a facade. Seth's life is anything but peaceful right now. I lean over and place a soft kiss to his cheek. His skin feels warm, but it's familiar.

"I love you," I whisper, before I turn back to my friends. "We need to go," I say.

Grace and Jamie follow me out of the hospital and once I am outside, I finally break down.

# 26

*Seth*

"I love you."

In my sleep filled haze, I swear I thought I heard Mia tell me that she loved me. I know I am just being delusional and hopeful, and maybe it was all the pain meds they pumped into me, but it was like she was really there.

Stirring, I open my eyes and see Brody sitting in a chair beside me. Looking around, I notice the stark white walls and the awful beeping noises that are making my head feel like it's been placed inside of a blender.

What the hell is going on? Am I dead?

"Where am I?" I ask Brody.

He stirs and I notice his face is as white as a ghost. He stands and slowly makes his way over to where I am laying on a bed. I feel a pinch and see an IV sticking out of my arm. My ribs ache and all at once, the memories come flashing back to me.

"Seth, you are in the hospital. I found you in your backyard. Someone kicked the shit out of you," he says, his tone serious and not at all light like it usually is.

Those guys must have messed me up pretty bad for Brody to bring me to the hospital.

"What about my mom?" I ask.

"She was here earlier. She had to go to work, so I told her I would stay here with you. Man, she is really worried about you. We all are," Brody sighs.

His words trigger a pain far worse than any ass kicking I could endure. I was letting everyone down and now I was worrying my mom. I felt like a failure.

"When can I leave here?" I ask.

"The doctor said that once you can stay conscious longer than five minutes, they can evaluate you for being discharged. They have been pumping you full of pain meds, so you have been out of it for two days. You have broken ribs. Seth, you have to stop whatever you are doing," Brody warns.

"Don't you think I know that," I say loudly, my voice horse. My throat is sore and my mouth is dry from being asleep for so long. I see a cup of water on the bedside table and I slowly lift my arm to get the cup. Brody helps me and I drink water for what feels like the first time in forever.

The water is refreshing and feels nice on my throat. I continue talking now that I feel like I am not dying of dehydration. "I am in way over my head, Brody. But, I just need five hundred dollars and I can pay off the rest of my debt. Once I get everything paid, I am done with gambling," I sigh.

"I'm glad to hear that, but you know I feel partly responsible for this mess. Let me figure out a way to help you out. Then, I swear, I will make sure those guys stay far away from the Raven bar and clubhouse and you," Brody insists.

I could fight him on this, but again, I know better than that. I need help and I can't be too prideful to not ask for help.

A nurse walks in and smiles when she sees me sitting up and awake. "Well, it's nice to see you finally awake," she says, with a cheerful tone. She's older, maybe in her fifties and her hair is almost all gray. She reminds me of my grandmother. "The doctor will be in here in a few minutes. Do you need anything?" she asks.

"No, I'm just ready to get out of here," I say.

She nods, before leaving.

"So, I had a crazy dream," I say to Brody. He gives me an odd look as he goes to sit back down in his chair.

"Those pain meds can really mess up your head," he laughs.

"Tell me about it. I swear, I dreamed Mia was here. It felt so real," I say.

My heart is burning as I think about Mia. I notice that Brody hangs his head for a minute and I realize something is up.

"What's wrong?" I ask him.

Running his hand through his hair, Brody lets out a deep breath before he looks back up at me again. His face is pained and he is starting to worry me. "Seth, it wasn't a dream. I called Mia and told her you were here," he says.

"What the hell, man," I shout. "Why would you do that?"

I'm beyond pissed right now. The last thing I would want is for Mia to know about this mess. She doesn't deserve this and I don't want her to see me in this low place in my life.

"I did it because she needed to know. Seth, you are falling deeper into a shit hole. If anyone could save you, it would be Mia. She was really worried about you."

"Mia has moved on, Brody. I don't need her worried about me," I say, tears burning my eyes.

I can recall only a few times I have cried in my life. All of them were when I was a young child, but right now, I feel like I could sob like a baby.

"Seth, Mia is not over you. Neither one of you will ever get over what you all shared. When she walked into this room, I saw nothing but love and fear in her eyes. Mia loves you, Seth, and you still love her, too," Brody finishes and crosses his arms across his chest.

He looks sly, but I know he is right. I do love Mia, but does she love me, too? I have to get out of this hospital so I can find her and figure all of this out once and for all.

# 27

## *Mia*

I find solace and peace in the strangest of places.

Take for example, the field that Seth and I had made our spot. It feels like a million years ago, but at the same time, it feels like just yesterday we were sitting in this open field together. A slight breeze flutters through my hair and I sigh, taking in the moment. I don't know why I came here today, or why I have been coming here for the last two days since seeing Seth in the hospital. Something inside of me brings me here, like I'm not even in control of myself anymore.

The first day I came here, I cried. I had fallen to my knees in the middle of the vast open space and wept so loud, I was afraid the heavens would hear me. The second day, I screamed. I allowed my anger to burst from within and I screamed and cursed everything I could think of. But today, I sit in silence. I just want to be at peace with everything that has happened.

Grace and Jamie had come with me the first day, but realizing this was a personal mission, they gave me the space I needed and didn't ask to tag along again.

Laying back on my elbows, I stare up at the baby blue sky as the white cotton-like clouds drift across the openness. I hear the roar of an engine, but I don't dare to look back. My mind has played way too many games lately, so I know better than to look back at the one lane road. Releasing a long breath, I smile to myself. This is the first time in forever that I have just been content with myself.

"Have you been here long?" a deep voice asks.

At first, I didn't dare to move. I decide I must be finally losing my mind and the delusions that Seth would be near me, have finally taken effect.

"I know you are mad at me, but if you would just let me explain," the voice continues.

Something deep inside my heart tells me this isn't some cruel illusion my mind has created. Slowly, I sit up before turning my head.

What I see behind me steals my breath and sends my heart racing at rapid speeds.

Seth.

I stand and I know he must be thinking that I am beyond insane as I just watch him without saying a word. He takes a step toward me, but I hold my hand, stopping him.

"Seth?" I ask, like I am still unsure if he is here or not.

Nodding he says, "Mia, it's me."

I can't explain it but something inside of me snaps at hearing my name cross his lips. He is here, just as he was really in the hospital the other day.

This time, I'm the one to move. My legs begin to race and as I close the distance between us, I leap into his open arms. My lips crash to his as a I close my eyes and take in everything that is Seth.

His arms fold around me and he holds me so tight, I'm afraid he might squeeze me to death. My hands play along his neck and into his messy hair that I have missed so much. He grunts, but all I hear is the beating of my heart inside of my chest. Everything about this is all wrong, but right now, neither of us care. It has been far too long since I have touched and held Seth.

Tears spring from my eyes and as I move my face away from his, I see that he too, has tears rolling down his cheeks.

"Seth," I begin, but my emotions overtake me.

"We don't have to talk right now," he says, taking his thumb and brushing a lone tear away. "Let me just look at you," he says, but I notice him wince as he speaks.

Suddenly, I remember that this incredible man was just in the hospital after getting his ass kicked. He has broken ribs and I just jumped right on top of him. I slide down his body, my hands tenderly touching his stomach.

"Seth, did I hurt you?" I ask, inspecting him.

A smile graces his lips as he attempts to hide the pain. "No, it's not too bad," he lies. "I would take whatever pain you give me, just to have you jump back into my arms again."

"You are insane," I laugh through my tears. When I take a step back, his hands grip mine like he is afraid that I will leave again.

"Possibly, but something told me that you would be here. I was discharged today, and I had to come here," he says, squeezing my hand.

"I did, too. This place is magical," I say.

"It's ours," he adds.

"Seth…" I go to argue, but he stops me by placing his fingers to my lips.

"We can talk about everything later. For now, just let me stand here with you," he says.

And so, I close my mouth and take in Seth. There is so much left unsaid between us, but at the same time, he is right. The painful and uncomfortable conversations can come later. We have both put ourselves through enough misery for a lifetime. The need to just be takes over and we are just us in our spot.

# 28

*Mia*

The sun begins to settle over the horizon some time later. All sense of time has escaped us. Seth and I sit side-by-side in the open field, both of us picking at long blades of grass.

The silence is welcome and nice and we both take it in as long as we can.

My phone vibrates and I see incoming texts from Grace and Jamie.

I see Seth's eyes narrow in on my phone at the sight of Jamie's name on my screen. I can already guess what he is thinking and I need to squash any arguments now. Shaking my head, I pick my phone off the ground.

"Seth, Jamie is my friend. She is Lana, Isaac's new girlfriend, niece," I state.

Relief floods Seth as he nods, like he wasn't just about to freak out.

"Wow, Isaac is dating," Seth says, chuckling a bit.

"Yeah, it's been pretty wild. I think they are getting pretty serious though. Lana has custody of Jamie and I have been showing her around Hollows Cove," I add.

"That's nice. Does she have a brother or boyfriend?" he asks me.

The question seems odd and out of place at first, but then I remember that Seth saw me and Alex on the ferris wheel. I can't help but laugh a little. "No. You can just ask me, you know," I say.

Seth doesn't say anything for a minute, but I can tell he wants to. After a beat, he finally says, "I know you saw me the night you were on a date," he says, venom lacing his voice.

I go to reach for his hand, but I wait. "Grace set us up on double dates. Turns out, Alex was also trying to get over a difficult breakup," I say, my eyes locking on his. "But, as nice as he was, there just wasn't a spark."

Seth eyes me carefully for a minute. "So, you aren't dating him?" he asks nervously.

"No. I haven't wanted to date anyone since you," I admit.

"Mia, I never stopped loving you," he rushes out, and my heart picks up beating rapidly again.

"Seth, neither of us ever fell out of love. I think that is pretty clear. But, being together wasn't right," I say, tears burning my eyes again.

I don't want to cry again, nor do I want to fight. But this conversation has to happen.

"I thought if I left, you would forget me. But, I just couldn't stay away," he admits.

"I could never forget you," I breathe.

Seth inches closer to me and I can feel his warm breaths on my cheek as he talks. "Mia, I know I fucked up. At the beginning, I thought I could keep everything simple. That I wouldn't get too far out of control, but I was wrong. All I wanted was to buy that warehouse so I could start a business and a life for us. I almost lost my life and I lost you," he finishes.

His words destroy me. I always knew that Seth wanted to do the right thing, it was just that his actions were all wrong. I can see the remorse he feels reflected in his eyes. He's changed and I can only hope that he continues to grow from this, because my heart can't stand to lose him again.

"Seth, you never lost me," I say.

His eyes widen before he crushes his lips back to mine again. We fall onto the ground and he rolls over on top of me. His body covers mine and I feel so warm and protected. I have missed this-- missed us.

"Where do we go from here?" he asks, as he lifts his head up for a moment.

"We go forward. We still have so much to talk about and there are changes that need to be made, but I can't walk away again. I promise," I say, before my lips find his again.

# 29

*Seth*

One week.

That was all it took for me to get my life back under control. After I left the hospital and found Mia again, we made a pact that we were a team. I ended up telling my mom everything. Brody had gone with me and to say she was pissed, would be an understatement. While she cried, screamed, and called me every name under the sun, she was glad that I was healing and making plans to right my wrongs.

I talked to the school and I could go back, but I would have a shit ton of makeup work to do. I didn't mind, really. When I told Mia that I had been looking at colleges before everything went to shit, she was beyond ecstatic. Once everything was settled, we were going to look at colleges together. I even apologized to Isaac for leaving town and not telling him I was quitting my job or that I was breaking his sisters heart. He was clearly angry with me, but he's in love now with Lana, so I think that softened his feelings a little. If he didn't have Lana, he would have probably killed me for everything I had put Mia through.

Can't say I would blame him.

Grace had threatened to kick my ass if I ever pulled another stunt like I did, and I swore to her I would spend the rest of my life proving to Mia and everyone else, that I was deserving of her love and acceptance. Grace seemed to relax a little, but I knew she would always have one eye watching me. She was a great friend to Mia and I wouldn't want it any other way.

Jamie was...interesting. This gothic chick definitely didn't fit the mold of girls in Hollow Cove, but she seemed to be protective over Mia, so I liked her instantly.

But Mia--her heart was too big and her love too forgiving. I didn't know why she decided to take me back or why she was devising the plan she was, but I would never stop thanking the stars and heavens above for giving me another shot with her. Mia was mine now and forever.

"So, how much money do you owe?" Mia asks me.

We are all sitting around Mia's living room. Isaac and Lana are out on a date and Brody and I are dirty and covered in grease from working on two more cars. I only need another four hundred dollars and my debt will be paid.

"Nope," I say, shaking my head. "I am not letting you get involved in this. I'm almost finished with these guys."

Mia gives me a frustrated look as she sighs. "We are all a team."

"Can't you just sell something?" Grace asks.

"I don't have anything but my bike, and honestly, it's not worth anything," I say, taking a sip from my bottled water.

"You all are depressing me and I am hungry. I will order a pizza," Jamie announces, standing and walking out of the room.

"There's another race happening," Brody begins. "You missed the last one since you were in the hospital," Brody trails off.

I know what he means, but there is no way I can take the risk again. It was because of gambling during the races that I got into this mess.

"What if I bet on you?" Mia offers.

"Hell no," I shout. I pull her close to me as we sit on the couch together. "I refuse to let you be part of that world. I love you for wanting to help me, but it's not up for discussion," I argue.

"We will see," she says, crossing her arms across her chest.

Something tells me, Mia isn't going to listen to me. Her stubbornness has always been a huge turn on to me, but right now, it is scaring the hell out of me.

Jamie walks back into the room and everyone is silent.

"What did I miss?" she asks, glancing around at all of us.

"Not much. Just Mia about to change everything," Grace says.

Jamie just shrugs her shoulders as she flops back down into her chair.

Mia's cryptic response seems to only further my fear that whether I like it or not, Mia is going to find a way to help me out of this mess.

# 30

*Mia*

Now that I have Seth back, there is no way that I am going to let him get hurt again. While my heart and mind is still angry with him for everything that has transpired between us, I still know that I would never be able to give my heart to anyone else. Ever.

I wish I could say that I had learned a lesson from Seth's near death experience, but if I am being honest, it only pushed me more to want to help him. When Seth and I had first started dating, we had gone to the Raven's Clubhouse and watched the races. While it was thrilling to watch, it was also a bit scary, too. I had seen the way Seth's eyes lit up with excitement when he rode his bike-- especially when racing. It was something ingrained deep inside of him and I would never want to take that away from him. However, the gambling was far too risky for him to continue.

I'm relieved once everyone leaves my house later and it is just me and Jamie left. Lana and Isaac aren't back from their date yet, so Jamie is stuck with me. I am still trying to get to know her more, so I think this would be the perfect opportunity to run an idea by her.

I need more ideas and Jamie seems like someone who won't hold back when asked a question.

"Jamie, I need to ask you something?" I say, as we busy ourselves with cleaning up the living room. Plates with pizza crust and napkins liter the room.

"Ok, shoot," she says, stuffing the pizza box inside the trash can.

Exhaling a deep breath, I lean up against the wall in the kitchen. "Well, I know you still don't know the entire story with me and Seth, but by now, you know he got into some trouble gambling and borrowing money from some pretty bad guys," I begin.

"Yeah, you told me most of it and then I picked up the rest from conversations tonight," Jamie replied.

"So, I need to help Seth find a way to get the rest of the money owed. If he doesn't have it soon, there is no telling what those guys will do to him next," I say, shuddering at the thought of someone hurting Seth.

"I understand, but Seth was pretty clear that he didn't want you to get involved," Jamie reminded me.

"Well, I don't always listen," I laugh.

"I am picking up on that," Jamie chuckled. "So, what do you have in mind?" she asked.

Smiling, I leaned in and said, "It will be our little secret."

****

Engines revved all around me as I stood in the last place I thought I would ever be.

"You know you stick out like a sore thumb," Jamie said, nudging my side.

My eyes grew wide as I turned to face her. "Seriously? You look like you should be in some goth film," I countered.

Laughing, Grace stepped in front of both of me and Jamie. "You both need to stay quiet. None of us fit in here, but arguing only makes us stand out more," Grace snapped.

Standing in front of the Raven's Clubhouse, I knew that what I was about to do was stupid, but I had no idea how mad at me Seth would be. My plan could work or it could blow up in my face.

Moving through the parking lot, I walked over to where I knew I would find Brody. Spotting us, he looked like he had just seen a ghost.

Brody came sprinting down toward us and met us halfway. "What the hell are you doing here?" he asked, looking around.

"I need to talk to you," I say.

"You couldn't call me on the phone?" Brody asked, clearly surprised by my presence.

Shaking my head no, I reply, "Not a chance. What I have to ask you requires an in-person conversation," I say.

Jamie and Grace stand beside me like my own personal bodyguards. I can tell Brody is nervous.

"Where is Seth?" he asks.

"Well, that's what I am here about," I say.

Sighing, Brody runs a hand through his hair. He looks up at the sky before meeting my gaze. "Something tells me I am not going to like what I am about to hear," he states in annoyance.

I can't help the smile that appears over my smug face. "I guess we will just have to see."

# 31

*Seth*

When Brody called and asked if I wanted to go to the races tonight, I almost thought I heard him wrong.

After everything that had gone down, I was sure I wasn't allowed to go to the races anymore. But, Mia was working and Brody insisted he wouldn't let me gamble.

Pulling up to the Raven's Clubhouse, I saw that the lot was packed. The races always brought in big crowds-- and big money. But, I couldn't think about that right now.

I just wanted to enjoy a good race with my buddy. I had tried to call Mia before I left my house, but she didn't answer. She must be busy, she will call me back later.

I park my bike next to Brody's and take my helmet off. The night is just getting started and there is an electrifying buzz surrounding the clubhouse. I can already hear engines revving and people cheering behind the bar and clubhouse.

"Calm down, man," Brody says, slapping me on the back. I can't help but notice that he looks a little nervous, too.

"It just feels strange behind back here," I say.

Brody nods in understanding. "I get it, but you aren't doing anything wrong tonight. This is just two guys hanging out tonight," Brody laughs.

I try to ease my mind and think about the next coming days that will be filled with work as I struggle to finish paying off my debt. Wait, oh shit.

I stop walking and feel the urge to scream. "Fuck!" I scream.

Brody stops moving and spins around. "What?" he asks.

"What if those guys are here tonight?" I ask. "I mean, they will surely be here collecting winnings and scamming more losers like me," I say.

How in the hell did I not think about this before? Of course, they will be here. Looks like my next ass kicking will be a public show.

"Seth, I swear I won't let anything happen to you," Brody says.

All I can do is hope he is right.

We start walking again and my stomach drops as I see the large crowd gathered around two racers.

The first race begins and my eyes are trained on my surroundings. I look for any sign of trouble, but thankfully, all I see are excited spectators. By the third race, I relax a little and even start to enjoy myself. The air is cool and crisp and the stars are shining bright in the sky. Maybe I was worried about nothing.

As the fourth race begins, something sparks my interest. A girl wearing a familiar looking helmet saunters up to the starting line. I hear guys whistling and shouting cat-calls as the girl stands before them. My heart begins to race and I start to shake my head. I look to Brody, but he refuses to look at me. I don't like the feeling that is beginning to stir inside of me.

However, it isn't until she takes the helmet off that I feel a fire ignite deep in my body.

The girl who is about to race is Mia.

My Mia.

What. The. Fuck.

# 32

*Mia*

My body is shaking and I can feel beads of sweat beginning to form on my forehead. I don't hear everyone around me, all I hear is the beating of my own heart. It is almost deafening.

If everything goes right, Grace, Jamie, and myself might just pull off this plan. When I had asked Brody to help me, he said no. It took some persuading and a big promise to never do anything like this again, but eventually, he agreed. I knew he didn't like my plan, but he also knew that this could be our only shot at helping Seth to get out of this disaster.

As I stood, waiting for the other racer to join me, I reviewed the plan in my mind. First, I would show up and surprise everyone by being a stubborn as hell female dead set on racing. Then, I asked Grace and Jamie to make sure that everyone bet against me. They worked the crowd while also staying away from Seth so they wouldn't get caught. If he spotted me, he would never let me go through with this. Finally, Seth would see me and stop me from racing. He would have to take my place, and of course, he would win. The money would be his and he could pay off the rest of his debt tonight. Now, all I had to do was wait.

****

It only took a second for Seth to find me in the crowd. Once his eyes locked on me, I knew it was now or never. Putting on a brave face, I stood strong as I watched the other racer walk his bike over to me. His smug grin had my legs shaking. He thought he had this win already.

"Mia!" I heard shouted over the noise around me.

I looked to my left where Grace and Jamie were watching. They, too, heard Seth calling my name. I nodded to them before turning my attention to Seth who was now bursting through the crowd. Brody was hot on his tail as Seth literally pushed and shoved people out of his way on his mission to get to me.

Once he reached me, I could see that he was seething mad. "What the hell do you think you are doing?" he asked me.

Gripping my arm, Seth yanked me to him. "Hey, stop!" I fought back.

"Mia," Seth growled out my name. "I know you are stubborn, but even this is low for you. What do you think you are doing?"

Holding strong, I raised my head and smiled. "I'm going to race tonight. Everyone is betting against me," I said proudly.

"No shit, they are betting against you. Mia, you have never driven a bike before," he yells.

"Hey, are we going to race or what?" the guy asks us. He stands next to his bike and I now notice that he looks familiar. I have seen him racing out here before. He see's Seth and his smile fades a bit.

"Yes, just give me a second," I say.

Seth's eyes grow wide. "Hell no, she's not racing. She doesn't even have a bike," Seth says, almost laughing now. "What's your plan? Are you going to race him on foot?" Seth asks sarcastically.

"No, I was going to use Brody's bike," I say.

Now, Seth whips his head around and I swear, I can see smoke coming out of his ears. "Brody!" Seth screams, and I see Brody wince.

"Someone better tell me what the fuck is going on before I lose my mind," Seth declares.

Brody gulps, fear taking over him.

"Seth, one of us has to race tonight. If it's not me, then who will it be?" I ask, raising my brows.

Seth stands in front of us stunned and confused. "Am I supposed to just stand here and pretend like I am going with all of this?" he asks, throwing his hands up in the air.

I take a step toward him and release the pent up emotion I had been holding on to. I know he is angry with me, but in time, he will forgive me. "Seth, I have looked the other way when you have asked me to. When you first started racing and borrowing money, I trusted you that things would work out."

Seth opens his mouth to protest, but I stop him. I continue, staring at him in his eyes. "Let me finish. I know that we can get your money tonight and never have to see any of this again," I say, waving my hands around. "Your eyes looking back at me now, tell me that you know what I am saying is true. Race one last time or I will race for you. Either way, there is a large sum of money on the line. Money that can fix this mess, but only if you swear here and now this will be the last time. Forever."

As I finish, I can hear the people around us growing frustrated with the wait. Seth's eyes never leave mine and when he opens his mouth, I say a silent prayer that he understands what I am offering right now.

"Brody, go get my bike. I have one last race to win," he says.

And, just like that, Promises in Hollow Cove were made.

# 33

*Seth*

I have no idea what in the hell has overcome Mia, but I can't say no right now. There is too much on the line for all of us. When this race is over, I am going to kill Brody and then have a very stern talking to my sexy and out of control girlfriend, Mia.

When I saw Mia standing there at the starting line, my heart stopped. It took me a moment to realize that I wasn't just imagining seeing her there. She is relentless, but damn if I don't love her for it.

Brody drove his bike over to the starting line and everyone jumped back. The guy who Mia was scheduled to race, now had an angry scowl covering his face. "What in the hell? Are you all scamming me?"

Shaking my head, I smile. "No, man. Look, I just found out about this myself. You can race the girl or me, your pick," I say.

"Can she even ride a bike?" he asks me.

"Only when I'm driving. With me, you will get a fair race," I add, sticking my hand out and offering to shake his.

He is reluctant at first, but eventually, he extends his hand and we shake like men. Everyone around us stares on in wonderment. Clearly, this night has taken an unexpected turn for everyone.

I throw my leg over my bike and sit down. Mia stands next to me, a triumphant smile on her face. I can't wait to do dirty things to that mouth later.

"Good luck," she says, winking before placing her lips on mine.

Her kiss takes my breath away, but as she backs up, I see nothing but love and admiration reflected in her eyes. This plan might be insane and risky, but I know that Mia wouldn't be doing it if she didn't think I was worth it. That we were worth it.

"I have you, I don't need luck," I say, before revving the engine.

Everyone backs away from the starting line and I take a deep breath as I ready myself for one hell of a race.

I look at the other racer and he nods, letting me know he is ready. A girl in a short, red skirt saunters in front of our bikes. She holds a checkered flag in the air and the crowd goes silent. There was a time when racing was everything I dreamed about. But now, all I dream about is Mia. She's mine again and I need this race now to make everything right in our lives. After tonight, no more racing, unless it's for fun.

The flag falls and the girl jumps out of the way. I take off and feel nothing but the cool air on my skin and the vibration of my engine as I seed down the track. I keep my eyes focused ahead, never once looking beside me to see if my opponent is keeping up with me. My bike is fast and as I push myself faster, my heart beats with a wild excitement.

Crossing the finish line, I breathe for the first time since starting this race. Slowing to a stop, I take off my helmet and access the race. My opponent is next to me and right now, I have no idea who just won.

Everyone in the crowd runs toward us and I see tears streaming down Mia's face. My heart drops to the pit of my stomach. I lost the race. And now, I am going to lose Mia again, too.

# 34

*Mia*

Watching Seth speed down the track has my heart stuck in my throat. I can't move or think. All I can do is watch and pray that Seth will cross the finish line first. Brody, Jamie, and Grace stand next to me and I can feel the nervous energy radiating from them, too.

This race is a defining moment in all of our lives. If Seth wins, his debt is paid off and we can move forward with our lives, never looking back. But, if he loses, we are taking a million steps backward.

I close my eyes for a second and then I feel Grace's hand on my shoulder. My eyes shoot open again and Seth is crossing the finish line. Did he win?

"Mia!" Grace yells.

"Did he win?" I ask.

"Hell yeah he won," Brody cheers, as he throws his fists in the air. He takes off down the track toward Seth and a wave of emotions crashes through me.

Tears begin to spill from my eyes as I realize all of the bad is now behind us. I'm beyond relieved and excited that Seth just won this race. My plan worked and now, we can take the first step into our new life together.

I take off running down the track along with all of the other spectators. Grace and Jamie are hot on my heels, but all I can focus on is Seth. He sits on his bike with a stunned look on his beautiful face.

When I reach him, I throw my arms around his neck, almost knocking him off his bike.

"Mia, what's wrong?" Seth asks. His eyes are wide and he drops his helmet onto the pavement below.

"Nothing is wrong. These are happy tears, you won!" I exclaim, crashing my lips to his.

"I won?" he asks, shock covering his face.

"Yeah, man. It's all over now," Brody cheers, patting Seth on the back.

Grace and Jamie stand beside us, smiles on their faces-- even Jamie looks happy.

Seth sighs and runs a hand through his messy hair. "Mia, I swear, I will never do anything to jeopardize our future again," he states. His arms snake around my waist and he pulls me to him. My hands fall to his chest and I can feel his heart beating like a drum in his chest.

"Hey, I 'm going to collect your winnings," Brody announces, before taking off toward the clubhouse.

Seth looks to me like he isn't sure what he should do. "Let Brody take care of it," I offer.

"I don't know how to thank all of you for what you have done," Seth begins. "I don't ever want to see those guys again," he finishes, releasing a deep breath.

"You don't have to thank us, just help me forget this all ever happened," I say.

"I will spend the rest of my life making sure this is nothing but a distant memory. Mia, you are my life now and forever. We will get married, have beautiful babies, and die together," Seth says, tears pooling in his eyes.

My breath catches as his sentiment makes me proud to call him mine. Sure, we have had our bumps in the road, but nothing can destroy a love like we share.

"Is this real life?" I ask, staring into the eyes of the man I love.

"No, it's our own fantasy. We are our own escape from reality," Seth stated. "A love like ours isn't one anyone else would understand."

He takes my hand and helps me on the back of his bike. My hands go to his waist and I love the familiar feeling of being on the back of Seth's bike once again. This is where I belong. Seth is my home.

"Where are we going?" I ask, leaning in to him.

"Our spot," Seth says, winking.

"Hey, wait," Brody yells, as he runs to us.

He stops in front of the bike, holding my helmet that Seth had made for me. "Seth, your debt is cleared. Now, we can forget about all of this," he says, handing me my helmet.

"My helmet," I say, taking it and placing it on my head. "Where did you get this?"

Waving his hands, Brody says, "Something told me you would need it. I brought it and stashed it at the Ravens Clubhouse."

"Brody, thank you for everything," Seth adds, smiling at his best friend.

"Go on, restart your love story," Brody says.

I look over to Grace who is crying tears of joy and Jamie, who watches me with happiness in her eyes. My life feels so complete right now with my new family surrounding us. I don't know what will happen in the future, but right now, all I know is that my life feels more complete than it ever has before.

Seth kicks the stand away and revs the engine. "You ready?" he asks.

"I've never been more ready in my life," I say, squeezing his side.

As we race off away from the track, I can't help but feel pure bliss as we make our way to the spot that has become our own. In Hollow Cove, promises were made and broken, but now, all of our promises will hold tight. Because for me and Seth, our love story is just beginning.

The End

# Extras

THE WOODSONG ACADEMY SERIES BOOK ONE
IGNITED
YEAR
W
ONE
ACADEMY
AMAZON BESTSELLING AUTHOR
LEIGH ALLEN

Check out the first two chapters of Ignited: Book 1 in the Woodsong Academy Series.

## Chapter 1

"Brie, are you up?" my aunt called.

"Yes, I'll be right down," I called back. I made a frustrated gesture as I threw on my black, Converse sneakers. I wasn't sure why she was rushing me. I still had another twenty minutes before I had to leave.

"You better hurry," she yelled, her hateful voice radiating through the walls of my bedroom. "If you think I am going to drive you to that supernatural Academy, you are crazy."

"I wouldn't dream of it," I mumbled to myself, in a flat, annoyed voice.

I glanced at myself in the mirror as I began to pull my shoulder-length, red hair behind my ears. My five-foot frame was short and slender, and my green eyes seemed to glow. Before walking out of my small bedroom, I glimpsed the photo—the only remaining picture—I had of my parents. I wished more than anything that they were still here with me. But they weren't. I was alone. It had been nearly five years since they were murdered and the supernatural police were no closer to finding their killers. I knew I would have to join the Woodson Academy alone, an orphan, and that alone made my anxiety increase even more.

You see, I am part of the supernatural world. A world where monsters from fairy tales and legends aren't just things of fiction-- but a reality. I had known since my birth that I didn't belong in the human world. My mother was a fairy and my father was a shifter. I would take on the abilities of my mother, which means I will become a fairy. When a supernatural becomes sixteen, they have to attend the Woodsong Academy to learn their true powers and find a way to live with them amongst humans in the human world. It was now my time, and my aunt couldn't be happier to get rid of me.

Unlike my mother, my aunt wasn't born with supernatural abilities. She had been angry and hostile over this for years. Hating my mother with an unfair, jealous rage. So, you can only imagine how frustrated she was when she learned that she was responsible for taking me in, five years ago.

Beep, Beep.

Outside my window, I heard the sounds of a car honking. Glancing out my window, I spotted a black van with dark tinted windows idling on the street. My stomach filled with nervous butterflies as I knew the van was here for me. I wish I could have had the orientation tour of the Academy like the other kids who would be attending, but I hadn't. When I was given the opportunity, my aunt refused to take me. She wouldn't dream of stepping foot into an Academy where she didn't belong. Her own selfish desires got in the way of doing what was best for me.

"Brie Bounty, get down here before they leave you here," my aunt called again.

Sighing, I rolled my eyes, grabbed the duffle bag that contained the few personal items and clothes I had, and rushed toward my bedroom door. Stopping, I quickly spun around and grabbed the picture of my parents before finally leaving my bedroom for the last time.

A sense of excitement and nervousness filled me. This was my new journey and as much as I wished I knew what to expect, I had no clue what was in store for me. All I knew was that I would be learning how to become a supernatural and maybe, hopefully...possibly find a way to track down the people responsible for my parent's death.

## Chapter 2

When I arrived at the school, I felt someone nudge my arm. I guess I had fallen asleep while listening to music. The ride had been long and I guess I had drifted off to sleep.

"Thanks," I said as I smiled. I looked out the window, but it was dark out now, so I couldn't really make out my surroundings.

From what I had read online, this school was secluded in a wooded area outside of a southern town. I knew I would attend school here and still learn everything I had in public school, but I would also learn about magic, using my powers, and how to transition back to the human world. More importantly, I would learn about supernatural Trackers.

Since my parent's death, I had conducted my own research about this 'group' of people who considered themselves the saviors of the human race. Their ultimate goal: to destroy all supernaturals. It was my belief that they were responsible for the murder of my parents. While there had been no real evidence pointing toward them, I knew in my heart and soul that it was them. My parents were good people and never had any enemies. They owned a small bakery in town and people loved them. When they had been found murdered inside the bakery, everyone was devastated. But me? I was beyond hurt. I was desperate for answers and revenge.

As I stepped out of the van, I held tightly onto my duffle bag and sucked in a deep breath. This was it. My chance to start a new life and finally get the answers I had craved for five years.

***

A set of thick, wooden doors opened as I stepped up to them. There wasn't anyone there, so I knew it was magic. As I stepped inside, the van pulled away from the driveaway and I realized it was just me now.

Walking inside, I could hear my footsteps as they clicked against the white marble floor below me.

"Welcome, Brie Bounty," a voice rang out to my left.

I whipped my head around and saw a guy around my age standing near a large, spiraling staircase. He had shaggy hair and dark brown eyes.

"Yes," I said, gulping.

"Hi, I am Ace. I will be your guide here at the Woodsong Academy. We have been waiting for your arrival," he said, matter of fact like.

I only nodded, unsure of what I should say. It was strange that he knew my name, but I guess that was to be expected. My arrival had been known.

I walked further inside the school and then I saw another person coming our way. Only, this was a woman who looked like she was almost walking on air. As she glided toward me, a soft smile graced her pale face.

Ace nodded and then turned on his heels to leave. He began to walk down a long, dark corridor and I rushed to catch up with him. Electra had nodded for me to follow him, and then had departed from the room we had once been standing in. Not wanting to be left alone in this strange place, I had no other choice but to follow Ace once again. We came to a long, spiraling staircase with black iron and deep mahogany stairs. The stairs looked as though they reached up to the sky above.

"So, are you a Witch? Trackers? Fairy?" I asked, as I followed him up the stairs. The questions tumbled out of me and I couldn't help but want to know everything I could.

Without stopping or turning around, Ace responded. "No, I am a shifter."

I just nodded to myself, unsure of what else to say.

We came to a stop at the top of the stairs, and I noticed several hallways branching out from the area at the top. Each hallway had a separate staircase leading to the next destination.

"Each supernatural group has their own separate wing of the Academy. Shifters have a hidden exit so when they have to shift and hunt, they can leave the building without disrupting everyone else. The Witches also have their own area equipped with a shield protected cement room where they can perform and practice spells without risking harm to the others. Finally, the fairies have their own section with access to additional windows and balconies where they can practice their flying and magic. From here, you will never enter any other coven. Since it has already been determined you are a fairy, you will go straight there. The others will each sleep in the main sleeping quarters until they are granted their true powers," Ace spoke. "Boys have one side of the wing and girls have the other," he finished.

"Ok," I said, feeling exhausted by the information and the walk up the stairs.

Everything about this place seemed so unreal. Ace continued walking until we reached a hallway that seemed simple in comparison to the rest of the Academy.

Everything about the place took my breath away. From the modern furniture and flat-screen televisions in the living area, to the chef style kitchen area that was modern and beautiful. I spotted doors all around the area, circling the living and kitchen areas.

"Inside each of those doors are bedrooms. You will live here until you turn twenty. Then, you will have to find your residency somewhere else in the world. This place will train you in your powers until you are able to live on your own as a supernatural," Ace stated.

He was turning out to be a pretty good tour guide. Too bad, I had about a million questions racing through my mind.

"Which room is mine?" I asked.

"This one," Ace said, pointing to the one to my right.

I walked to the room by myself and opened the door. Inside was a large, black, iron canopy bed and a dark wood dresser. I had my own bathroom and a closet filled with clothes. The only thing missing was the personal touches that made the room special to each individual person.

"This is really nice," I said, admiring the space. I only had a small room at my aunt's house, and she never would have bought me such nice furniture.

"Well, we do enjoy our luxuries," Ace chuckled.

"What about you?" I asked, feeling the heat rise to my cheeks. I hated that Ace had that effect on me.

"I don't stay here with the other students."

"Ok," I simply said, looking everywhere other than at Ace.

"I will leave you to rest for a while. At dinner, you will be called down to join everyone else," he said, before closing the bedroom door behind him.

I didn't even have time to ask when dinner was. Ace just seemed to disappear. He was a strange guy-- hot, but strange. Without knowing what else to do, I fell onto the soft mattress of the bed. The silk, gold-colored sheets felt like feather kisses against my warm skin. I closed my eyes and sighed. I was finally home.

www.ingramcontent.com/pod-product-compliance
Ingram Content Group UK Ltd.
Pitfield, Milton Keynes, MK11 3LW, UK
UKHW022018190726
13853UKWH00005B/1988

9 798774 279692